To Barb

Best Wishes

Evelyn

Printed 1999
In the United States of America
by White Birch Printing, Inc.
Spooner, Wisconsin 54801

ISBN 0-9670655-0-X

To order, contact:
Evelyn Safeblade
W8504 Jellen Road
Spooner, WI 54801
Phone (715) 635-7536
$6.00 + $2.00 SH

Chapter 1

She was pretty in a petite way with dark curly hair falling to shoulder length, innocent blue eyes and small trim figure, except where the obvious evidence of pregnancy was displayed. A condition more emphasized than six months would usually portray due to her small boned frame and prognosis of twins.

Ann Randall sat alone in the doctor's office, supposedly waiting for his return, but in reality too numb to be even aware that he had been called out on an emergency. Her husband, of only a few short years, was dead, drowned in a silly, freak accident in Lake Hebron just off the Hampton, Illinois shore. According to the story told by the policeman who had brought her to this huge metropolitan hospital, Tom had died at eleven o'clock at night while his two companions, men Ann didn't even know, tried valiantly to save him.

The doctor returned, moved swiftly behind his desk not bothering to sit down, knowing he would only have to rise again before many moments passed.

"Are you feeling better, Mrs. Randall?" he asked, not unkindly, just abstractly. A man with hundreds of patients needing his care.

Unable to speak, Ann nodded.

"Here are some sleeping pills. Take these tonight. Tomorrow is time enough to make arrangements." As a last act of concern the doctor helped Ann to her feet, walked her to his office door and directed a white uniformed nurse to call a cab.

Jolted back from a zombie state, Ann protested silently, I can't afford a taxi! Tom and I are saving to buy a house, pinching every penny to get out of that apartment. Then it came to her, Tom and I, there will be no more Tom and I. Meekly she allowed herself to be placed in the cab, gave her home address, hunted in her purse for enough money and when they arrived, paid the driver. Alone, she went into her dark first floor apartment.

It wasn't strange that she thought of money before she thought of Tom; that is all she had been doing lately, thinking of money. Planning their escape from the ugly, almost windowless apartment where only two windows on the front of the building abutting the sidewalk and one at the rear allowed any daylight to filter in. Three story touching tenement buildings lined the neighborhood streets. Front doors opened onto cement sidewalks which ran to the curb, giving no room for even green weeds to grow.

This was not a neighborhood of crime; it was rather a neighborhood of defeat where just a few of the young dreamed of better ways to live. Everyone worked, except the very old and very young but their jobs were minimum wage or slightly above with the result that the ever rising cost of food, shelter and gas kept them all stagnant.

Ann automatically turned on the hall light, which was needed day or night, bolted the front door and dropped her purse on the nearest living room table. The room was exactly as she had left it: terribly neat, drab and gloomy. She sat heavily on the nearest living room chair and burst into tears.

"OH, Tom, Tom," she cried.

Visions of how he had looked the night of their high school prom flashed across her mind. Those few strands of brown hair that wouldn't stay in place and kept falling across his forehead, the special light in his eyes when he looked at her and that adorable smile. They had pledged their love to each other, forever, as the band played a soft waltz and he held her in his arms.

"Why, why did it happen? They had been working so hard to make their dream come true. Together they had saved ten thousand dollars over three long years. With his job as a mechanic at a local gas station and her position as a typist in a small office, they had worked at saving, even collecting pennies. Yet, in one night, in one brief moment, their dream was gone! She was alone! And in three months she'd have two babies to raise in an old, depressing tenement on her five dollars an hour salary.

Ann wiped her tear drenched face, went to the desk and rummaged around for the address book. I have to call Tom's brother, she thought and Aunt Eva in Pinewood and Sally Canfield. I'm sure Sally will call the office for me and tell Mr. Appleby. Oh, and the gas station. Where is that number? And what time is it in California? I can't call Timothy Randall in the middle of the night.

Doing the simplest thing, like finding a phone number, seemed to require the greatest effort; Ann doubted she had the ability to cope.

Down Funeral Home on Asher Street handled the funeral. The few neighbors Tom and Ann knew attended the service along with the men from the gas station and the women from Ann's office. Tom's brother had come from California, leaving his wife, children, new baby and aged mother at home. Ann's only relative, an aunt living in Wisconsin, was unable to come because she had to care for her wheelchair bound husband, crippled with arthritis.

After the service and a brief luncheon at the local church, everyone left, leaving Ann and her brother-in-law to return alone to the apartment and begin the sad task of rearranging lives.

"Did my brother leave you any insurance?" Timothy Randall asked, as they sat in the apartment kitchen eating one of the donated casseroles.

Ann pushed a piece of chicken around the plate with her fork, having no desire to eat even though the food looked and smelled delicious.

"There is a thirty thousand dollar policy from his job and I think there is a five thousand accidental death that goes with his medical insurance," Ann answered listlessly.

"That's not very much these days," Timothy said

frowning, envisioning an additional dependent.

Ann watched the concern cross his face. He's so like Tom, she thought, able for the first time since the tragedy to see beyond her own problems. Only Timothy is serious and responsible, lacking that fun loving quality that made Tom so delightful. Poor Timothy, he's already caring for Mother Randall, besides his wife and three small children.

"Ann, why don't you come out to California and live with us? You can't stay here alone. We'll be a bit crowded but we'll manage. Our three children can share the back upstairs room."

For a moment she pictured their modest four bedroom home, now occupied by six people. Where could they possibly house another person? No, three other people, she speculated, glancing down at her own bulging frame?

"No, Timothy. You're so dear to offer but you have enough with your own family and Mother Randall. I'll manage somehow."

A momentary straightening of his shoulders indicated the relief he felt. However he bravely continued, "How can you cope with the babies coming?"

"My office insurance will pay for the doctor bills and the hospital and I'm entitled to six weeks maternity leave. After that I'll just have to find a cheaper apartment and a good baby sitter.

"A less expensive apartment! I'm sorry if I sound as if I'm insulting you, but do they come any cheaper?"

"You're not insulting me." Ann gave a hollow laugh. "I hate this place. It's so dark and dreary inside and outside there isn't even a spot for a few flowers, never mind a tree or a bit of lawn. However it does have two bedrooms. I should be able to find an equally unpleasant one bedroom apartment somewhere for less."

"It's not just these four walls. What about the neighborhood? You probably shouldn't be out alone after dark."

"There are still enough old immigrant families here, good hard working people who keep their teenagers in line. I think it is safe enough, though I admit I don't go out by myself after nine o'clock at night."

"I still don't like the idea of you raising a family here. It's one thing to think of you and Thomas living here until you saved enough for a house, but it's something else to think of you living here with young children. Ann, with only your salary, you'll barely have enough for food and a roof over your head," Timothy persisted, unable to shake off the feeling that centuries of male ancestors were looking down on him with disfavor.

"I know, Timothy, but perhaps I can get a better job or something. Please could we go to bed? I'm really all in."

"Of course. You must be exhausted. But promise me you'll come to California if you can't manage."

"Promise."

Chapter 2

Timothy left the next morning, still serious, still worried about his brother's wife. In addition to her financial problems, she would have to face her first birthing alone. Ann had assured him that her good friend and coworker, Sally Canfield, would be with her. In fact, Sally would move in the week before the babies were due, but still it seemed wrong to him somehow that no family member would be there to give her support.

As Timothy's cab pulled away Ann had a moment of sheer panic. A desperate feeling of loneliness swept over her. All those fun times she and Tom had had together when they were first married crowded into her mind. At the beginning he had always been there: laughing, joking, teasing her about her little worries, bringing her flowers and insisting they drop everything to go dancing or to the movies. There would be no more dancing, only worries.

Forcing herself to put aside her fears, Ann dressed in a light cotton skirt and blouse and with savings book secure in her purse, left for the nearby branch bank. She was determined to clear her financial obligations. The funeral had to be paid for and the florist bill taken care of. No matter how one felt, the currency exchange went on. For services received, money had to be paid. It mattered not at all to the dollar signs whether the bill was for a funeral or a new car, they were still the same dollar signs and decimal points.

Already the Hampton June sun was oppressive, heating up brick, cement and asphalt, still warm from yesterday's rays. In spite of the heat it felt good to be out in the morning air, away from the muggy dampness of her enclosed apartment.

Old men and women and young children were gathered on the front stoops on the shady side of the street. "Sorry to hear about your husband," the old people commented as Ann passed.

"Thank you," she responded. Stopping now and then to ask of family matters, she worked her way to the end of the street.

The branch bank, around the corner on Asher Street, was quiet at nine-thirty on this work day morning. Mr. Brinkman, a bank officer, noticed Ann's entrance and came to greet and console her. Leading her to a seat beside his desk, he waited until she was seated, then sat at his desk and gave her what he felt to be an encouraging smile.

"I'm so glad you're free, Mr. Brinkman," Ann said hurriedly. "I do have some questions about how to proceed. You see, I need to pay the funeral bill and as it's quite large, I'll need to take the money out of our savings account."

"How much is it?" he asked kindly. Mr. Brinkman had helped Tom and Ann set up their house savings account and had become fond of this "sweet young thing," as he thought of Ann from his advanced years.

"Five thousand, thirty dollars," she answered bravely, mentally slicing their savings account in half. Three struggling years to save ten thousand dollars, half of it gone in one day!

"No problem. A cashier's check would be best. Made out to Down Funeral Home, I presume."

"Yes."

Mr. Brinkman typed for a moment, then handed her a paper. "Just sign here," he said, pointing with the tip of his pen. "Good, that's all settled. Here is your cashier's check. Now, do you mind if I ask you a few personal questions?"

"No."

"Did Thomas leave a will?"

"Yes, we both made out simple wills when we were first married, leaving everything to each other."

"Splendid, then all you will have to produce is a death certificate and a domiciliary letter. The death certificate Down Funeral Home will obtain for you. The domiciliary letter comes from the court. Our bank lawyer can help you with that, if you need help."

"Oh, thank you, Mr. Brinkman. I had no idea how to go about obtaining the necessary papers."

"No problem, no problem. By the way, did Thomas leave you any life insurance?" he asked hopefully, with an expression that indicated he dreaded the thought of yet another young mother going on the dole.

"Yes, a thirty thousand dollar policy is guaranteed and there should be five thousand from his medical insurance." Strange, Ann thought, when you're dealing with money and legal matters you become devoid of feelings. Just a little nervousness from concentrating on what needs to be done, otherwise nothing.

"May I make a suggestion?" Mr. Brinkman asked in a serious tone.

"Of course," Ann replied, rather curious as to what his suggestion might be.

"Unless you have bills to pay with the thirty thousand dollars, I suggest you put the money in long term government bonds. The thirty year bonds are paying fourteen percent right now. Naturally they may go up with inflation the way it is today but still fourteen percent is a very nice return. It will give you four thousand, two hundred dollars a year for thirty years, with no risk at all. All the way to the year 2009."

Almost half my yearly salary, Ann speculated in wonder, having been employed the last few years as file clerk and typist at five dollars an hour.

"That sounds very wise," Ann responded. "How do I go about purchasing government bonds?"

"This bank is able to obtain bonds from the Federal Reserve Bank," Mr. Brinkman replied.

"Can you purchase the bonds for me?"

"Certainly, we'll be glad to make the arrangements. There is a slight fee of twenty-five dollars that this bank charges for the transaction, but we can take care of that matter very nicely. You just send the insurance company a copy of the death certificate and the domiciliary letter with an accompanying letter. They should send you a check within a few weeks," Mr. Brinkman answered pleasantly. He was relieved that Ann seemed to have some common sense, wasn't going to plunk the money down on clothes or some foolishness and wonder later how to pay the grocery bill. You never could tell with young people these days.

"Then everything is all set?" Ann questioned, securely locking the massive cashier's check in her purse.

"Let me buzz Mr. Jenson, our lawyer. If he's in the office, perhaps you could see him while you're here. Get everything under way, so to speak."

While he waited for the inner office phone connection, Mr. Brinkman added casually, "At least Thomas' car loan hasn't yet been approved, so you don't have to worry about car payments."

"Car payments, what car payments?" Ann questioned in shock, quickly losing her facade of business like composure.

"Yes, Jenson, have one of our young clients here, Mrs. Randall. She needs help with obtaining a domiciliary letter. Good, good, I'll send her along in a minute."

Mr. Brinkman replaced the phone and addressed Ann. "Well, that's fortunate, Mr. Jenson can see you right now." Mr. Brinkman smiled a complacent smile, quite satisfied with all the help he was giving this "sweet young thing." He was sure his wife would be impressed when he told her this evening of his benevolent endeavors.

"Didn't Thomas tell you he was buying a new car? Perhaps it was meant as a surprise," he added casually, secure in the knowledge that the bank's funds were safe, the loan not having reached the stage of actual transfer.

"No, no, he didn't," Ann responded, now trying to reason out what must have been going on, while following Mr. Brinkman to the lawyer's office.

"No harm done," he assured her. "Though Thomas probably put a deposit on that Thunderbird at Honest Freddy's. You should be able to get the deposit back."

Ann followed the lawyer's instructions: paid the funeral bill, obtained several copies of the death certificate, and too exhausted to understand or confront Honest Freddy, headed for her dreary home.

At five-thirty, Ann was drinking a cup of instant coffee and still trying to figure out what had gone wrong with her marriage when her friend Sally Canfield arrived carrying two bulging suitcases.

"Thought you needed me as much now as when the babies are born." Sally said. "So I've come to spend the week with you. Besides, Aunt Lidia is visiting Mom and if I get out of the way they can have a good time without thinking of feeding me every night."

Sally dropped both of her cases in the hall passage way.

"You're right, this is a dismal place," she added, surveying the kitchen, then glancing out the back door at the small yard with its erratic patterns, formed by a variety of clotheslines. Brushing back loose strands of straight brown hair, Sally sat on a kitchen chair, kicked off her working heels and asked forthrightly, "How is it going? If you want to cry all night just put me in the back bedroom."

"Have you had dinner?" Ann asked, noting Sally's tailored business suit. Aware that her friend discarded her work uniform at the first opportunity, preferring jeans and sweat shirts on her slightly plump, five foot five inch frame.

"No, and I'm starving. I'll settle for an omelet if you are up to doing any cooking."

"You set the table and I'll even add a tossed salad."

"Heavens, sounds as if we're dieting," Sally moaned, rising to hunt for dishes, napkins and silverware. "By the way, you haven't answered my question," she added, scrutinizing her friend and fellow office worker.

"I don't know how I feel," Ann said slowly, continuing to beat eggs. Pausing to place the frying pan on the stove, she tried to be honest about her feelings, both to herself and to Sally. "At first I was devastated. I cried and cried. Then it began to dawn on me that I was weeping bitter tears almost more for my lost vine covered cottage, my own security, than for the loss of Tom."

"You didn't see much of him lately, did you?" Sally asked, never one to back off from her forthright manner.

"Well," Ann said hesitantly, wondering whether to mention the surprising information that Tom had been in the process of buying a new car. "He needed time to have fun, to be with his friends. We were working so hard to save money for a house."

"Ever since he knew about the babies coming, he suddenly needed time with his buddies?" Sally voiced her skepticism.

"We didn't exactly plan to have a family so soon, as you may have guessed. We wanted to buy the house and have it furnished before starting a family. Add to that the fact that I have old fashioned ideas about raising children and you can imagine there was some conflict."

"I thought you had started looking at houses? What about that one on Vine Street you mentioned last week? Victorian wasn't it, with a wrap around porch?" Sally asked, while preparing coffee and plugging in the coffee maker.

"Oh, that was a nice house, lots of lovely carved woodwork in the living room and on the stairway. But the real estate agent said the electrical wiring would have to be completely redone and those high ceilings would increase the heating costs. I did see a cream colored Cape Code on Oak Street, near the grade school, that I liked. I had an appointment to see it next week."

"Then you had the money for a down payment. You and Tom could have afforded a house, even with the early arrival of your family."

"Oh, yes. We had ten thousand dollars in a special house account. Plenty for a down payment and the bank would give us a thirty year mortgage. It wasn't a question of affording the house."

"Still, you're talking about a lot of expenses to take on all at once," Sally said contemplatively.

Ann served the omelet. "I gather you think I was pressing him too hard, what with wanting a house and wanting to stay home with the children for the first few years," she said defensively, speaking her own fears.

"Don't ask me," Sally said laughing, bringing some lightness to the moment. "Just getting married is too much pressure as far as I'm concerned. I'm for Mom's cooking, cleaning, and neat laundry after a day of typing up insurance forms."

"Do tell me about Aunt Lidia. You haven't mentioned her before," Ann said, feeling the need to change the subject. While talking she placed the tossed salad and some crescent rolls on the table. The meal looked quite appetizing for one so hastily prepared.

"She's Mom's younger sister and just a

sweetheart. Unfortunately she lives in Massachusetts so they don't get to visit very often. When they do get together, I might as well disappear as they have a million things to say to each other and a hundred things to do. I don't want them changing their schedule for the working girl in the family and I knew you needed me. So here I am."

"Thanks, Sally. You're a sweetheart. I do need help."

After eating, Sally and Ann agreed they would go through Tom's possessions and ready his clothing for a donation to a nearby church rummage sale.

"We'll do it right away," Sally insisted. "If you don't, you won't be able to face the task in a few weeks. Right now you're numb; you really don't believe he's dead."

Ann winced at the blunt words. Giving Sally the back bedroom with its one window, Ann settled herself in the middle windowless, extra bedroom and storage place. Surprisingly, she fell asleep quickly, her last thoughts, a decision to put Sally against Honest Freddy.

All Saturday morning they worked diligently packing and sorting. Ann had done this hundreds of times, making decisions as to what garments needed washing or mending, which items should be sent to the cleaners or discarded, so that this task she had dreaded was similar to past Saturday mornings and not too difficult to manage. Only when she was packing Tom's favorite robe did she break down and let the tears flow. Without a word Sally took over, sending Ann to prepare coffee while she finished the box and sealed it securely with tape.

Some items Ann even kept: a number of sport shirts to wear around the house over her bulging abdomen, thus saving her few maternity clothes for the office, and four pairs of jeans that had been too small for Tom, but fit her nicely before the pregnancy.

"Good for you," Sally said, noting the saved clothes. "No point in being squeamish when you need every bloody penny you can get your hands on."

They packed the boxes in Ann's ten year old Volkswagen bug. Once Sally was assured that the car would actually get her to the church and back, she willingly drove to nearby Saint Francis while Ann remained to prepare a quick lunch.

Over egg salad sandwiches and milk, Ann described her strange conversation with Mr. Brinkman about the down payment on a new Thunderbird at Honest Freddy's.

"Tom planned to buy a Thunderbird! Gosh they're expensive!" Sally Canfield exclaimed, her eyebrows rising.

"I know, I know."

"How much do you suppose Tom put down?" Sally wondered.

"I have no idea."

"Boy, we're not leading from strength on this one." Sally sighed heavily. "I've heard stories about Honest Freddy. It may be hard to get the money back. But let's give it a try. Why don't we whip over there right now? I'll drive and do the talking, you just appear as pregnant as possible. Wear that blue thing, it makes you look as if you need to head for the hospital within minutes."

Once in her blue maternity outfit, (which up until Sally's remark, Ann had thought attractive,) Ann climbed in the passenger seat of her Volkswagen, glad not to have to squeeze herself behind the ever closer steering wheel.

Departing from her usual casual attitude of, "Do it yourself; millions of women are pregnant," Sally became all solicitous once they stepped through the door of Honest Freddy's show room. Taking Ann's arm she lead her carefully around shining new cars to the elaborate office.

"Honest Freddy, I'm here to help this grieving young widow, Mrs. Thomas Randall," Sally began as she helped Ann into a leather chair in plain view of the showroom floor. Handing Ann a large white handkerchief, for any critical juncture during the negotiations, she continued, "So sad, so sad. Here they were, this loving couple, planning on finally having one of your beautiful new cars. When suddenly tragedy struck him down before their moment of joy. He was drowned, wiped out in that cruel Lake Hebron."

Honest Freddy's built-in smile and confidence seemed to fade with Sally's opening remarks. Retreating behind his desk, a cautious expression replaced his hardy manner.

"The deposit, you know," Sally suggested.

For an agonizing moment, Honest Freddy remained quiet, observing Sally. Finally he opened a desk drawer and extracted a ledger. Looking through his book, Honest Freddy found the Randall account and said with an attempt at renewed cheer, "Yes, we have it right here. Two hundred dollars on a new Thunderbird."

Two hundred dollars, first hurdle overcome, Ann thought. Good for Sally, she's doing splendid work though she's putting it on a bit thick with that "moment of joy."

"Of course, a Thunderbird may be beyond your

means, under the circumstances," Honest Freddy continued, addressing Ann with what he felt was a sympathetic voice. "But we have some wonderful smaller, er, less expensive cars. The two hundred would be a nice deposit on one of those. Come, let me show you a special blue compact, just right for you. It's a steal, really. Should cost hundreds more, but we like to save a few cars for friends. Helps them get back on their feet, so to speak." Rising from behind his desk, Honest Freddy straightened his tie and prepared himself for the job he knew best.

Quickly intervening before he could get into full stride, Sally murmured sadly but rather loudly. "Oh, the bills, the bills this has caused. I just can't think of any way out for my poor friend here. One so hates to turn to bankruptcy."

Realizing this must be the time for the white handkerchief, Ann dutifully dabbed her eyes. Fortunately, just at that moment, an older couple in the showroom happened to glance her way. Aware of the older couple's curiosity and potential buying ability, Honest Freddy ungraciously took out his check book.

"We usually don't return deposits," he warned them sternly, "but under the circumstances." Without continuing, he quickly wrote out a check for two hundred dollars and leaving them unceremoniously, went rapidly to greet the older, prosperous appearing couple.

Sally dutifully helped Ann to her Volkswagen Beetle. Not until they were out of sight did Ann break into giggles. "Sally, you were marvelous!"

"Wasn't I though. I should get a job there. I could show him a thing or two about selling cars. Of course it helped my case to have a grieving, obviously pregnant women in the background."

"That older couple peeking in the office window didn't hurt either," Ann reminded her friend.

"We deserve a reward for that show," Sally announced. "Can you afford a cup of coffee and a donut?"

"Under the circumstances, I think I can just swing it," Ann agreed.

They spent a pleasant hour lingering over brewed coffee in a cozy little shop and then headed for the apartment and an inexpensive Saturday night of watching television.

On Sunday they prepared and froze evening meals for the coming week. Ann and Sally would be returning to work on Monday. Sally moaned over the thought that her mother, Agnes Canfield, would not be waiting with luscious dinners at the end of their working day, but acknowledged one had to make sacrifices for others now and then.

At nine o'clock on Monday morning Ann once again sat at her typewriter with insurance billings piled to her right. The typewriter seemed miles away as Ann pressed her ever expanding bulk against the desk. Aware of her dilemma, Mrs. Smith, the other office worker and Sally suggested Ann switch to filing and sorting the mail while they handled her typing chores.

If their boss, Mr. Appleby noticed, he made no comment. A bachelor in his sixties and the oldest of eight children whose mother thought it unseemly to appear in public after the fifth month, poor Mr. Appleby was frankly over his head. His only remarks to Ann, whom he now avoided looking at, was to remind her that she had six weeks maternity leave coming.

I know, Mr. Appleby, Ann said to herself, each time the reminder was given. But like a gold bar, I'm hoarding those weeks for desperation time. Smiling at the anticipated relief poor Mr. Appleby would feel once she was gone, Ann politely followed his work directives, always given with his eyes glued to the floor or the desk top.

At the end of their week of apartment sharing Sally packed her bags and returned to her window lit, cheerful home and her mother's cooking. Before leaving, promising to return a week before the babies were due.

For the second time Ann felt desperate loneliness. Somehow losing Sally's frank, honest concern, and cheerful companionship with all the everyday household duties, was worse than losing Tom's restless impatience with domesticity.

Get hold of yourself, Ann demanded; Sally has her own life to live. As sweet and as kind a friend as Sally is, you cannot lean on her. You must face life alone.

Chapter 3

Returning from work the following evening, Ann noticed two boys about ten years old, playing catch. Playing ball, what a nice thing for boys to be doing, she thought, watching their concentrated efforts to catch the ball in obviously borrowed, oversized baseball gloves. Before the thought left her mind and before she reached her own front door, a squad car pulled up and a gruff masculine voice said, "No playing in the street." Silently the two young boys retreated to one of the front doorways and sat dejectedly on the front step. The police car drove on.

Oh, how sad, Ann reflected. It's such a good thing for children to play athletic games, but where in this neighborhood can you play ball safely? The back yards are all too small. They're barely big enough for garbage cans and clotheslines, never mind play areas. The only open space is the dangerous street, between the parked cars.

Ann seethed with frustration. I must escape, she decided. This is no place to raise children.

Once inside her apartment, she bolted the front door and headed wearily for the kitchen. The phone rang, sending a sharp sound through the dreary rooms.

"This is Aunt Eva. Ann, dear, how are you?"

"Aunt Eva, so good to hear your voice!" Ann exclaimed. "Where are you calling from?"

"Home in Pinewood. I started worrying about you down there all by yourself. Are you all right?"

"I'm doing okay," Ann replied, trying to sound convincing.

"You poor dear. I wish I could come down to Hampton and be with you, but that's impossible."

"I know you do, Aunt Eva, but just knowing you care, helps."

"What about your coming up here? Could you come up over the Fourth of July? We'd love to see you," Aunt Eva asked, sounds of hope in her voice.

"Why yes, yes I could," Ann replied, her spirits lifting. "I'll take my last personal day on Friday and be with you on Friday night."

"OH, how wonderful! I'll write you the directions," Aunt Eva responded, now quite cheerful.

The thought of a long weekend in the country with trees and flowers and acres of green grass sent Ann humming happily to prepare her dinner.

Just last year Aunt Eva and Uncle Albert had retired to a small Northern Wisconsin town when Uncle

Albert's arthritis forced him to be confined to a wheelchair. They had purchased a small ranch home on a village lot in the tiny hamlet of Pinewood. From Aunt Eva's description, there were seventeen homes clustered around a town square, one church and a combination restaurant, grocery store, gas station and general meeting place on the main road through town.

Checking to see that she could manage the space between the seat and steering wheel, Ann, assured she could still drive, packed her suitcase and impatiently worked at the office until Thursday evening.

Sally and her mother were spending the weekend at a resort where they could play golf and be waited on by a competent staff. Delighted that Ann would also be vacationing, Sally bid her a cheerful goodby, promising to share lunch on Tuesday when detailed reports of their respective vacations could be given.

Too excited to sleep, Ann left Hampton, Illinois at four o'clock on Friday morning. The weather report had been for clear, sunny conditions with the temperature climbing into the high eighties. Not until she crossed the border into Wisconsin was Ann able to see the surrounding countryside. The first rays of daylight lit up the farm country with a soft pink glow, outlining red barns, silos and white farm houses nestled in stands of tall trees. Fields of corn, wheat and alfalfa stretched for miles around them.

After the Wisconsin Dells the four lane highway climbed rolling hills, dipped into green valleys, sending Ann eagerly on to the next spectacular view. Slowly traffic thinned making the driving easier, giving Ann plenty of time to absorb the beauty of the surrounding countryside. Past Tomah she hit a stretch of tall stately pines, majestic in their quiet dignity. Stopping at a Wisconsin roadside for an early picnic lunch, she breathed in the cool air coming down from Canada and felt her spirits rise. To her long starved love of nature, every crow, every ragweed, every thick leafed milk pod was beautiful.

By two o'clock she was approaching Pinewood, a much earlier arrival than Aunt Eva was expecting. Hoping that her aunt wouldn't mind, Ann came to the Pinewood sign and turned off the highway. On her right was the village square, containing a few gigantic shade trees and a large surface of mowed grass. She drove by a small white frame home, a two story yellow house and coming to a cream colored ranch house among maples, birches and pines, knew that she had arrived.

The Gilberts were in the side yard, Uncle Albert in his wheelchair watching his wife pull weeds in a border of geraniums and day lilies. Hugs and kisses were given in greeting. After Ann was shown her room, the three spent a relaxing afternoon in the shaded yard, catching up on family news while Ann absorbed the quiet tranquility of a summer afternoon in the country. The Gilberts' home was small but marvelously compact with every inch of space efficiently used. Best of all it had numerous large windows, giving Ann a view of a cluster of spruce from her small middle bedroom. The fresh, clear night air allowed her the best nights sleep she had had in months.

Following a breakfast of bacon and eggs, welcomed by the hunger country air produces, Ann washed up while Aunt Eva saw to Albert's needs.

Outside the sun was shining. Blue jays flew back and forth from one leaf covered tree branch to another. The smell of flower blossoms drifted through the kitchen window.

"Do you mind if I take a walk?" Ann asked, eager to

explore the village and the surrounding countryside.

"Of course not," Aunt Eva answered. "Do you good to get some exercise. Will you stop by the store for a gallon of milk on your way?"

"Will do," Ann agreed. Going quickly back to her suitcase, she put on her most comfortable pair of sneakers.

The road beyond the park became a gravel track leading westward. Shortly buildings ceased. Now on both sides were farm fields, stretches of woodland and lush swampy areas. Ann had walked about a mile, the last part gradually uphill, when she came to a clearing on her right, evidently an area that had been the center of a farm. Walking up the grassy driveway she saw the remains of what must have been a house, of which all that remained was the outline of a rock foundation and a few charred beams, barely visible through the natural growth that had reclaimed the land. Off to her right, a shed or small barn remained, gray, weather-beaten, but sturdily upright. Further to the right, nestled in a group of trees and unseen from the road was a dark brown log cabin, obviously of new construction, for the ends of the logs were smooth and unpunctured by bugs or rot. A "For Sale" sign nailed to one of two large oak trees near the log cabin gave Ann the courage to investigate. The thick oak door was locked, but the two casement windows on the south side did not contain curtains or shades. They gave Ann a view of the interior when she pressed her face to the glass.

Inside, the foot wide logs were in their natural color, covered only by a coating of clear varnish. There was only one room, completely bare except for a sink directly under a south facing window and an old fashioned cook stove situated toward the back of the building. The cook stove was resting on a small brick floor that overlaid the hardwood floor visible in the rest of the room. A pine paneled wall seemed to close off one small section on the west side, no bigger than a storage area. The back wall was an uninterrupted expanse except for a door located in the middle. It was all so simple, yet beautiful. But what sent Ann's heart beating rapidly was a large window on the east wall, framing a peaceful forest scene of white pine, spruce and maple. To her mind the thick massive logs meant protection and security and the view through the east window, peace and tranquility.

Ann's mind remained centered on the snugly built cabin as she walked the mile and a half to the store, purchased the milk and returned to the Gilberts. She had mentally built in a sleeping area under the huge window, shelves for canning supplies against the back wall, and a desk facing the south window before she told Aunt Eva of her discovery.

"The Anderson place," Uncle Albert said when Ann described her marvelous find. "The main farm house and barn burned down five years ago. Alma Anderson moved into town after the fire, into that neat white house across from the church. She gave the farm property to her son, Roger. He built that cabin in 1976 so it's new and in good condition."

"Why is he selling?" Ann asked.

"He took off for California about three years ago, just after he finished the cabin," Uncle Albert replied.

"It's a darling place. Wouldn't it be a great place to raise children?" Ann asked.

"Perfect," Aunt Eva agreed enthusiastically. "The land is nice and high and the soil is good for gardening."

"Seth Ruffles gave Roger a hand with the construction

so you can be sure the best of material went into that place," Uncle Albert added.

Though Uncle Albert was crippled from arthritis, unable to use his hands or legs with any efficiency, Ann was glad to see that his speech and mind were intact and that the couple's close companionship remained in spite of his handicap. Together they planned their little garden, shared the village news, helped at the church and consulted each other on home improvements and upcoming menus. Of one mind, they agreed it would be wonderful if Ann could purchase the Anderson property and raise her children under their watchful assistance.

"Do you think there is any chance I could look inside the cabin sometime today?" Ann questioned.

Going to the phone, Eva said eagerly, "I'll call Alice Ruffles. Her son has the listing." After hearing a one-sided conversation, the two impatient listeners were informed that Alice's son was showing some other property, Alice herself was canning peas, but her brother, Seth Ruffles, would obtain the key and meet Ann at the Anderson property in half an hour.

"Don't let Seth Ruffles disturb you," Uncle Albert warned. "He doesn't say much and always looks as if he would like to bite your ear off. Good soul, nevertheless. Farms a spread about two miles down the road from the Anderson place."

An old battered pickup truck was waiting in the sandy drive when Ann reached the log cabin. Dressed in farmer bib overalls and a faded blue shirt, Seth Ruffles, somewhere in his early seventies, fit Uncle Albert's description perfectly. Ann tried not to be intimidated by his sour expression and said cheerfully, "It's so nice of you to take the time to show me around."

Seth didn't bother answering. Selecting a key from a collection, he opened the front door. Inside the thirty by thirty foot room looked the same as it had through the window. It housed a cook stove, a sink, and bare log walls.

"How is the wiring?" Ann asked, recalling all the articles on advice to home buyers that she had read in women's magazines.

"Ain't none."

"No wiring!" she said in surprise. As Ann spoke, she glanced around the baseboards in the entire room. Not one wall plug came into view. His two word statement was unfortunately true. "However do you light this place or plug in a refrigerator?"

"Kerosene lamps. The creek."

Kerosene lamps, Ann had heard of, always prefaced by "back in the old days." However the reference to the creek was beyond her. "What do you mean, the creek?"

"Put your milk in a bucket in the creek. Keeps it cool. One back the other side of the barn," he answered, his longest sentence so far.

Ann still didn't understand but let it pass. Going to the sink, which had no faucets (just what appeared to be a hand pump on one side,) she raised and lowered the handle several times. Nothing happened, there wasn't even a trickle of water.

Reluctantly she asked, "How do you get water?"

"Needs to be primed. Ain't been used in a year," came his gruff response. Without further comment he left, leaving Ann staring at his retreating frame. Shortly he returned carrying a pail of water. Pouring water down the top of the pump he worked the handle vigorously. Within a minute a steady stream of clear cold water poured from the trough into the sink and disappeared down the drain.

"May I try it?" Ann asked, intrigued. She wanted to make sure that this wasn't magic he alone could produce. Pumping rhythmically she was able to keep the stream of water running. Pleased with this simple accomplishment, Ann turned to inspect the area behind the partition, leaving the strange stove for later ignorant questions. The small enclosed space contained a porcelain bath tub with legs and a toilet. Delighted at seeing this modern convenience, Ann, still true to tips for home buyers, pushed the flush handle. Always flush the toilet, making sure the plumbing is in good working condition, the articles had repeatedly instructed. The result of her moving the handle was only a slight clicking sound, no running water gushed forth, in fact, on inspection she saw that there was no water in the bowl. Completely at a loss, she turned to Seth Ruffles, aware for just a second of the trace of a smile crossing his otherwise ugly face.

"Got to fill the tank."

"From the kitchen pump," she added, beginning to be wise as to the lack of modernization. "The tub too, I suppose," she said, noting the two holes where faucets were usually found.

"Yep. Connected to the septic system though, required by law."

"Why is Mr. Anderson selling?" she asked, still avoiding the mysteries of the stove.

"Sold some writing to them T.V. people. Went to California."

"Oh, what show does he write for?" Ann questioned, quite intrigued.

"Don't know. Never watch the tripe."

"Oh."

Unable to think of further questions, Ann approached the stove wearily. A thick pipe extended from the back to a metal protected hole in the roof. A wire handle protruded part way down the pipe, within easy reach. The back of the stove was quite high, containing two sections at the top which opened to reveal storage space. The entire stove was solid iron, a black mass that must weigh a ton.

Now seeming to read her mind, Seth said "Oven" when she opened the biggest door and "Wood box" when she opened a smaller one on the left side. "Hot water," he added when she looked at a metal box attached to the stove with a spigot at its lower end. Reaching up he took hold of the wire handle protruding from the stove pipe. "Draft," he said turning the metal handle back and forth.

This time she caught a full grin as it crossed his face. The old goat, she thought, he's having a grand time, probably can hardly wait to tell the folks at home about the dumb city girl.

A gold finch flew past the picture window, landed in a maple tree and turned his head to survey the occupants inside. The tiny yellow bird renewed her courage.

"How much is he asking?" she inquired. "And how much land goes with the house?"

"Twenty acres. Farm lands been sold, only woods, marsh, and creek left. Twelve thousand."

Twelve was too much. Ann's heart sank. With the five thousand from medical insurance and a little over five thousand dollars still in their savings account, she couldn't possibly offer more than ten thousand dollars. If only she could buy this place, there would be no expenses other than taxes and Uncle Albert said they were about two hundred dollars a year. With the income from the thirty year bonds, surely she could afford the taxes and be able to purchase what food she couldn't raise herself. There would be no water bill, refuse bill, phone bill or electric bill and best of all, if she could manage, a beautiful place to raise her children.

"I'll offer him ten thousand dollars," Ann said determinedly.

For the first time Seth Ruffles lost his contemptuous composure. His thick eyebrows rose a half inch in surprise. Looking at her obvious pregnancy, he commanded, "Your husband has got to see it!"

Ann couldn't resist, in one swift remark she paid him back for all the secret smirks she had witnessed that afternoon. "Ain't got none."

To her surprise, Seth looked shocked, then burst into uncontrollable laughter. A laughter so infectious she couldn't help but join in. When he could speak he said, "You mean, in your condition, you want to split wood, trim wicks and wash over a scrub board all by yourself? Why, aren't you something!"

"It's so beautiful here. I just love all the trees and wild flowers and birds and the sweet smell of the air. This would be a wonderful place to raise children," she said sincerely.

Going outdoors, Ann stood in the front yard and breathed deeply. The intense summer sun was blocked here and there by protective trees, merely in patches did it reach the ground and heat up the grass and sandy soil.

"Will you show me the land?" Ann asked, turning to her elderly real estate agent.

At the mention of land Seth's stern frown returned.

"Suppose you'll want all the apples," he said, as if the purchase was all but assured.

"What apples?" she questioned.

"These here five apple trees," he answered, pointing out healthy looking trees filled with little green apples, on the further side of the outbuilding. "I've been spraying them," he added, giving her a side glance.

"Of course, if you've been caring for them you must have some of the apples," Ann acknowledged. Until now she was unaware that apple trees needed spraying and furthermore had no idea how difficult a task it would be to care for such trees. "If I buy this place, would the apples from two trees be a fair deal?" she asked.

"I'll even throw in some honey as well as doing the spraying for two trees," he agreed, his good humor returning.

Willingly Seth showed her the woods, the swamp; where baby ducks were raised in the spring and Canadian geese rested in the fall as well as the small running stream where she could keep butter, eggs, and milk cool during the hot summer months.

They parted, sure of a beginning friendship. Seth to relay her purchase price, Ann to describe to her aunt and uncle the wonder of her possible, very own home. True, she would have to learn pioneer ways to survive, but as yet she was too elated to appreciate the work involved, so joyously returned to the cream colored ranch house.

It wasn't until late that night, when she experienced a vivid dream of herself and two babies huddled under blankets slowly freezing to death that woke her in terror, did Ann realize the implications of what she had undertaken. "What am I doing?" she asked herself as violent chills ran through her body. "However can I raise two children out in the woods with no electricity, no hot water and no plumbing?"

Glancing at her wrist watch in the glow of moonlight that shone through her window, Ann saw that it was two o'clock in the morning. She eased herself out of bed so as not to wake her aunt and uncle, wrapped herself in her too small robe and stood by the window. Visions of her ugly tenement apartment filled her mind – the hot water that ran from the faucet, the toilet that flushed, the heat that came on with a turn of the thermostat. With each thought her home became less dreary, the neighborhood less depressing.

Yet here in Pinewood bright stars filled the still, night sky, undimmed by gaudy electric signs. A three quarter moon shone on the peaceful landscape, outlining the blue spruce along the edge of her relative's property in black and white. A small dark animal scurried into sight, then disappeared in the undergrowth, unconcerned with Ann's dilemma.

However does one saw up enough wood for the winter, her mind questioned as her subconscious absorbed the peaceful scene. Seth Ruffles had said there was plenty of dead wood on the property, but how much did you need? Surely this meant buying an axe and a saw. What about those apples on the three remaining trees, how did one preserve them? Apples didn't last more than a few weeks in the refrigerator, that she knew and she wouldn't even have a refrigerator. Searching her mind, Ann tried to recall the stories of pioneers she had read in school. Men fighting Indians, hunting wild turkeys, driving wagons over the prairies. What ever did the women do? How did they store food, wash clothes, make clothes, clean and cook? The books seemed to have glossed over the contributions of women. No answers came to mind.

Somewhat reassured by the quiet beauty outside, Ann crawled back into bed. The hopeful thought that Roger Anderson would turn down her offer of ten thousand dollars allowed Ann to doze off and on the rest of the night.

Chapter 4

Coming into the kitchen the following morning, Ann brushed aside a lock of her curly black hair and headed straight for the coffee pot.

Noting her blurry eyes and down cast expression, Uncle Albert said accusingly, "You didn't sleep very well last night. You wouldn't, by any chance, have that old illness, buyer's remorse, would you?"

"Afraid so," Ann admitted, smiling weakly.

"Don't you worry, you've made the right choice. Greatest place in the world for children," Uncle Albert said reassuringly.

"But I don't know a thing about living without modern conveniences!" Ann explained, holding her coffee mug with two hands, as if its warmth would reassure her.

"Eva and I remember a few things our mothers and fathers used to do. We could probably come up with the answer for most problems," Uncle Albert replied, persisting in his belief that country living was the right answer.

"I agree with Albert," Aunt Eva said as she rolled out a pie crust. "Ann, would you mind getting out the cereal while I finish this apple pie and get it in the oven?"

"I'll be glad to," Ann replied. "I'll serve the juice and make the toast as well. In fact, why don't I take charge of breakfast? You have your hands full with baking."

"OH, that would really help! You see, the pie has to be finished before church so that we can take it to the after church pot luck."

"That sounds great! Do you have pot lucks every Sunday?"

"We have them once a month, on the first Sunday. Then we sometimes have them on special occasions like christenings and wedding anniversaries," Aunt Eva answered. Opening the oven door she placed the pie on the middle rack. Turning back to clean up the counter, she added, "You know dear, Albert is right, this is a lovely community for children. And there are enough old timers in this village, plenty of them will know the old ways. They didn't get electricity up here until the forties."

The congregation of the village church did appear to be made up of a goodly percentage of retired people, a few in the middle years and a fair amount of younger families with small children. Ann was introduced to Phyllis Westland, a young farm wife who was expecting her first child. They liked each other immediately and knew, given the opportunity, that they would become good friends.

Aunt Eva explained, as they slid into the last pew beside Uncle Albert's wheelchair, that only a few young women actually lived in the village. One was Holly Fines, who with her husband Donald, ran the combined gas station, store and restaurant. Donald was sitting in the front pew, he and Holly taking turns attending church while the other cared for their business. The other young families were either farmers or business people who worked in Hendersonville and preferred living in the country on five to twenty acre parcels of land.

Reverend Woodbind, a pastor in his late fifties, approached the lectern and smiled at his congregation, before opening the Bible to the first lesson.

Ann hadn't been to church for years; it has been so easy to find an excuse not to go. But when the little congregation stood and sang lustily, "Jesus calls us o'er the tumult of our life's wild, restless sea," Ann began to feel that she belonged, that she was part of the group. I'm not alone, she thought, as the musical words, "Day by day his sweet voice soundeth saying, Christian follow me!" drifted to the rafters. I don't have to struggle all by myself. With this thought came her first awareness of genuine inner peace.

Following the service the congregation moved to a side room next to the sanctuary. Here long tables were set up for dining. The women assigned to serving placed hot dishes, salads, rolls, relishes and a variety of vegetables on the dining tables, while the rest of the congregation selected seats.

Reverend Woodbind welcomed their visitor to the church, making Ann feel especially included. After grace was given the meal began. Bowls heaped with home cooked goodies were passed back and forth until emptied, then refilled to begin their journey again. Amid forks full of ham, chicken and scalloped potatoes, church matters were discussed. The Johnson's farm house had been damaged by fire, did the ladies quilting group have enough quilts made to give them three? The old church stove would soon need to be replaced, could the men hold an auction or some other benefit to raise the money? A liturgist was needed for the Sunday after next, could someone volunteer?

Ann looked around for Seth Ruffles, knowing he lived alone, she assumed he would be at the pot luck. "Where is Seth?" she asked his sister, who happened to be sitting across the table.

"He isn't much for church, since his wife died. Though he sure got a kick out of showing you Roger's house," Alice Ruffles answered. "First time I've seen him laugh in months."

This comment didn't reassure Ann, but too polite to quibble she let it pass.

Questioning her aunt later she did learn why Seth and his married sister had the same last name. "Alice married a distant cousin," Aunt Eva informed her. "Lots of Ruffles in this part of the country, bound to have a few marrying each other, now and then."

The news came while Ann and her relatives were leisurely resting in the side yard, too full after sampling numerous dishes to rouse themselves from lawn chairs. In the light of day Ann's fears had subsided, as they usually do when the sun shines. So the shocking fact that she would soon be in possession of one unmodernized log cabin, an outbuilding and twenty acres of land, did not throw her into a complete panic.

Then too, there had been that moment during the

church service, during the time of silent prayer, when she had felt reassured. As if God was truly with the congregation in that simple little church. In wonder and comfort she held that memory in her mind.

On Tuesday morning, refreshed, rested, displaying a tan below her dark curly hair, Ann arrived at the office. Sally Canfield was already typing. Her straight brown hair, which usually fell across her face in an uncontrollable manner, was pulled back tightly, secured by two buns at the back of her neck. With her classic Nordic features, the new, severe hair style gave her a strikingly sophisticated appearance. Added with the new coiffure was delicately applied makeup and a new tailored dark brown business suit. Ann wasn't sure Sally still existed until a wink from recently elongated lashes reassured her. Impatient for lunch hour, Ann could hardly wait to discover what had brought about this transformation.

As soon as Mr. Appleby and Mrs. Smith left for a nearby restaurant, Ann and Sally unwrapped their sandwiches, secured cups of coffee from the office coffee maker and started talking.

"Sally, you look like a sophisticated business woman, absolutely stunning! That suit is perfect for you, slims you down and gives you that look of class." Ann said, her eyes full of admiration.

"The new me," Sally responded with delight. "All thanks to you, a down payment on a Thunderbird and Honest Freddy."

"How did you come up with that?"

"Mom and I spent the weekend at Adlers, which is a very plush resort. We wanted to treat ourselves to a few days of gracious living. Adlers has swimming pools, golf courses, tennis courts and gourmet restaurants. It was divine! Anyway we were seated with this couple at dinner one evening when the lady mentioned that their son was having trouble with a car salesman. Naturally we got to talking about car dealers and I related our encounter with Honest Freddy. I must have made an impression for this lady, Mrs. Allen, invited me to apply for a job at her business. Ann, she has her own company, a cosmetics concern that earns millions of dollars a year! And she is looking for an assistant sales manager for the upper Midwest states. The position pays thirty thousand dollars a year plus a bonus. Can you believe it! I'm going for an interview on Thursday. If I get the job, I'll see if I can find one there for you. They are bound to pay more for good office help than Mr. Appleby. Mrs. Allen is charming and delightful but best of all she is confident, a woman that commands respect. Oh, how can I describe her! She is just like all the self-assured business men you see, only she is a lady at the same time. Mrs. Allen has become my roll model, my idol, my goal. I'm on my way to make millions!"

"Sally, that is wonderful! I'm sure you can do it. You have already made a great start with the way you look," Ann said, pleased with her friend's new enthusiasm and challenging plans for the future.

"If it all works out, you'll come with me, won't you?" Sally asked. "I'm sure I'll be able to secure a position for you in Mrs. Allen's company. You're really the best typist we have here when you can get close enough to the typewriter. You're sure to be welcomed at Mrs. Allen's Cosmetics. And just think, with a better salary you would be able to afford a decent apartment and a good day care center for your kids."

"Sally, you old sweetheart. You're always so kind and thoughtful. You're the dearest of friends. But I'm taking

-40-

a different route," Ann replied, a touch of sadness in her voice as she spoke the last few words.

Sally waited, her happy expression changing to one of concern.

"I bought a house in Pinewood," Ann stated simply.

"You bought a house! With what?" Sally asked in complete astonishment, not believing for a moment that what she was hearing could possibly be true.

"Not exactly a house. A log cabin for ten thousand dollars. A lovely new log cabin with foot thick walls and nestled in a grove of pines, maples, and birches."

"Ann, you can't buy a garage in a decent neighborhood for ten thousand dollars," Sally protested.

"You can in the country. Oh, Sally, it's all by itself on twenty acres, just surrounded by wonderful trees, wild life, flowers and green grass. The cabin in on a dirt road where there are so few cars going by that you can see deer tracks in the sand and even a real woodchuck or possum crossing the road. I just came alive with all the loveliness."

"I can see you came alive, you look quite healthy after your weekend in the country. But how are you going to stay alive? The simple matter of money, my friend," Sally questioned, now convinced that this was an impossible dream. One of those wild ideas that hit people whenever they vacationed some place where the scenery was exceptionally beautiful. Sally always thought of it as the desert island syndrome.

"I'll have the interest from my bonds and if I can raise my own food, cut my own wood, sew our clothes, and supply my own water, I think I can do it."

"Wait a minute! Your own wood, your own water! Let's have a complete description of this dream house in the northwoods," Sally insisted.

"Okay, okay, I'll heat with wood, there are plenty of dead trees on my twenty acres. All I'll have to do is saw it up in the proper lengths and transport it back to the cabin. My light will be from kerosene lamps and candles and my water from a well. There is an old fashioned hand pump by the kitchen sink. All you have to do is prime it and keep pumping and you have an endless supply of free water. The result will be that I'll have no bills except two hundred dollars a year for real estate taxes and something for insurance."

"I'm going to a plush glass tower on Superior Avenue and you're going back three generations," Sally said, looking absolutely disgusted.

Ann laughed, "I'm doing the same thing you are. I'm becoming an independent woman who is going to control her own destiny."

"You're a nut really, but I'm with you. I'll keep a pair of old jeans and a sweatshirt in my car - hidden of course - for my visits to you. Two women taking charge of their own lives. Let's hope neither one of us falls on her face."

Chapter 5

Starting one hot, muggy July evening Ann began the process of selecting the items she would take to Wisconsin and marking the furnishings she would leave for the sale. As she would have very little room in her new home, her take selection had to be carefully considered. Everything must be useful.

In spite of the summer heat she inspected blankets, sheets, towels, kitchen pots and pans, assorted silverware and everyday dishes, listing each item she intended to take in a small notebook.

Abandoning her check list at ten o'clock for a cool coke before retiring, Ann noticed her neglected mail. There was a chatty, encouraging letter from Aunt Eva and Uncle Albert, a brief note from her brother-in-law (oh, dear, she had better write soon and tell him of her plans,) two bills, one the electric and the other the refuse pick-up, several advertisements and a letter from Beverly Hills, California.

Surprised, not knowing anyone in Beverly Hills, Ann ripped open the envelope. Halfway down the page of legal sized, yellow lined paper was a short message:

> Glad you can't afford to modernize.
> Root cellar in small barn. Trap door
> in barn floor.
> Roger Anderson

What a blunt statement, Ann thought. How does he know I can't afford to modernize? And if he knows, what a horrible thing to write, as if he's happy I'm poor. Besides he must be paid by the word, he certainly didn't waste any with this message, not even a salutation. Thank goodness he can build better than he writes letters. Roger Anderson may be the village hero to all of Pinewood, but as far as I'm concerned he can stay in California.

Throwing the brief note in the waste basket, Ann went to take a refreshing shower.

Sally's interview with Mrs. Allen went well. She would be starting her new career in a month, the exact time Ann would be beginning her new life in Pinewood. On hearing their news Mr. Appleby became very depressed, quite obviously much more so over losing Sally than losing Ann. However, Mrs. Smith knew two older women who would be glad to take their positions at the same salary and on being informed of this fact, Mr. Appleby's disposition improved tremendously.

"All is splendid," Sally remarked happily, during one of their lunch breaks. "Power to the brave and courageous. We have a month to get ready. You help me buy a stunning wardrobe and I'll help with your sale and get you moved to Wisconsin."

"That sounds marvelous! But it isn't quite fair," Ann answered. "You'll be doing ever so much more work for me than I'll be doing for you."

"Nonsense! I'll talk Jimmy Burns into moving your things in his truck. He can take whatever you need in the northwoods, up some weekend. He loves to fish, so that will give him an excuse to try out the lakes up there."

Poor Jimmy, Ann thought, he's still caught up in a one-sided relationship that has gone on since grade school. He fell in love with Sally in the third grade and has been in love with her ever since, even though she never seems to return his devotion.

"If Jimmy is willing to do that, he can stay at my log cabin. That would at least save him the expense of overnight lodging."

"He'll be more than happy to run up to Wisconsin, if I ask him," Sally replied with a knowing smile. "As far as the sale goes, I love house sales, they're great fun. Besides it will be good practice for me, a warm up for my future occupation. Furthermore your helping me shop will be good for you. Running around to the upscale shops and seeing nothing but stunning outfits will give you something to dream about during those long cold winter months when you'll be spending your time stoking the wood stove and shoveling snow."

Ann laughingly reminded her friend, "You'll dream about clothes too when you find out the outfits, from the places you intend to shop, will cost half your new salary."

"Ug, suppose you're right. How we sacrifice to advance in the world," Sally mused, munching on a tuna salad. Weight watching having been added to her career preparations tasks. "Well, let's get down to business. We have two weeks left in July and one in August. If you can get your things ready for a house sale the last Saturday in July, I'll have Jimmy drive up to Wisconsin that same weekend with the stuff you want to keep. This coming weekend we can put all the sale items in the two front rooms and do the pricing. The first week in August you can stay with Mom and me, that way you won't have the August rent to pay. How does that sound?"

"Perfect, we can shop the week I stay with you. By that time I'll be all settled, leaving my mind free for fur coats, cashmere sweaters and alligator bags," Ann replied.

"Careful, you'll spend my whole future salary, not just half," Sally cautioned.

Selecting the middle windowless bedroom for the items she would ship to Wisconsin, Ann packed her everyday dishes, fortunately a plain white setting for six, the twelve pale gold plastic glasses she bought at a sale and all her cooking utensils. In a large cardboard box went four wool blankets, six bottom sheets and six tops, twin bed size which would fit nicely the three serofoam, five inch mattresses she would order from Sears. The mattresses would be piled one on top of another making a couch under the picture window, for use during the day and three beds for sleeping when the children would be old enough to need regular beds. This meant that she would be selling all the furnishings from both apartment bedrooms as she had plans for built-in storage at the cabin, therefore no need or room for dressers and vanity tables. In fact the only furniture she decided to take was the round formica topped maple kitchen table and the four matching captains chairs. Gambling that she would make enough on the sale to afford lumber for the planned built-ins and thus have a more efficient home than regular furniture could provide. All electric lamps would have to be sold, all pictures, absolutely no room for those. Besides her pictures would be the country view from three windows, charming enough to rest any weary soul.

Determined to take only one box of books, Ann selected the Bible, her best dictionary, two books on gardening she had just purchased, a home repair manual, five cook books, and six novels, three by D.E. Stevenson and three by Miss Read, a book on wild flowers and a paper back, "Birds of North America." Of their sports equipment she kept only the two fishing rods and tackle box.

Taking every candle from its holder, Ann packed these in two shoe boxes, along with one wooden holder for the three inch candles and one pewter holder for the rest. Having always loved the soft glow of candlelight, Ann's two boxes were barely able to hold the assortment of half burned and new candles in her collection. These she placed in the trunk of her Volkswagen beetle, along with a flashlight; items she wanted to make sure she could locate quickly.

Finally she carefully packed a box with a few pictures of Tom, four selections from Mother Randall's antique glassware and her own Mother's cameo brooch, all that remained from her own family after fire destroyed her parent's home. This box would be carefully stored in the barn for the day when her children were old enough to learn about their ancestors.

By the third evening, when she had finally finished,

there were just seven cardboard boxes, two fishing rods, one second hand play pen and one table and chairs in the spare bedroom. A meager beginning for a new life.

The first weekend was hot and sticky, the temperature approaching ninety-five degrees with the humidity oppressively high. Sally and Ann longed to be in an air conditioned house or high in the mountains where cool breezes would sweep over their hot bodies, but they diligently worked instead, cleaning out the back bedroom, stacking the sale items around the living room and dining room. On Sunday evening they had everything tagged and ready. Mother Randall's remaining antiques had been priced by Ann's retired neighbor, who had previously been in the second hand business. They were quite pleased when they saw thirty and forty dollar signs on fancy glass pitchers and ornate plates.

"At least two hundred dollars on glassware alone," Sally said happily, placing her lovely legs, clad in cut off denim jeans, on the arm of Ann's sofa.

Sipping an ice drenched coke, while wiping her dripping forehead with a wet washcloth, Ann was glad their labors were over. True she would be sleeping on a mattress thrown on the floor in a bare back bedroom for the next week, but who cared, maybe it would even be a little cooler without all the furniture absorbing heat.

"I've got to take a shower," Ann said wearily.

"Go ahead, you first," Sally agreed, downing her coke in two swallows. "Enjoy the luxury, won't be long before you're bathing in a metal tub."

"I have a bath tub," Ann said with dignity. "No running hot water, but a tub. Just picture me with a fishing rod in my hand, pulling in a walleyed pike from a crystal clear lake, while you're in some stuffy hundredth floor boardroom, all metal and plastic, listening to some aged windbag go on and on about talcum powder."

"Stop, stop or I'll drop everything and go with you," Sally said laughing. "The only thing that keeps me here is knowing I'll be wearing a Chanel suit and silk blouse when I'm in that stuffy boardroom. Maybe even driving home in a Mercedes after the meeting."

Miraculously, after two weeks of boiling hot sun and wilting temperatures, the day of the sale dawned cloudy and dark with the promise of rain. At nine in the morning, when Ann opened the door, a long line of people eagerly pressed forward. Most lived in the surrounding tenement district and were anxious to purchase household items at second hand prices. Ann heard Sally carrying forth, now in her element. "That table would be lovely by your window and wouldn't this antique vase just set the whole thing off. With the money you'd be saving on this table you could easily afford a nice antique touch. And of course, over the years it would increase in value. Such a comfortable sofa and hardly a bit of wear. I'm sure it will go within half an hour at this price.

Leaving Sally in charge, Ann sat at the money table, taking payments and watching her furnishings disappear out the front door. Even reducing the price on a lamp when the buyer, a thread bare old lady, fumbled in her purse to find change enough to make five dollars.

Right behind the old lady was a fourteen year old boy, looking nervous but determined. He placed Tom's ice skates and hockey stick firmly on the money table and carefully drew out folded bills from his back pocket.

Ann stared at the skates, scuffed and worn from years of use but perfectly sharpened and suddenly there was no sale going on, it was just she and Tom in their apartment and he was at the door dressed in a winter jacket with the hockey stick over his shoulder and his skates dangling from the extended hockey stick. She heard him say, "I'll be back about eleven," with an expression of anticipated pleasure on his face.

A middle aged man's voice brought her back to reality. "My son is determined to play hockey," he said apologetically.

Forcing her mind to pay attention to the man and boy before her, Ann noticed that the father had immigrated from a warm climate and his son's interest in ice hockey seemed to bewilder him.

She forced a smile as she took the boy's money. "A lot of high school boys are into ice hockey," she said, trying to reassure the father.

The boy left quickly with his prize, before his father might have second thoughts.

As they left Ann thought, Tom's skates just went out the door and I don't feel any grief, any sadness, any heart breaking loss. There is just pain, she thought in astonishment, not the pain of loss, the pain and anger when something goes wrong, seriously wrong.

"Are you taking the money?" a gruff woman's voice demanded.

"Oh sorry, sorry," Ann said falteringly.

She reached in the precious money box for change for the impatient woman while telling herself firmly; put away your marriage, your relationship with Tom. Forget it, it's over. Think of your children, think of the future, only the present and the future.

By late afternoon the crowd was thinning. Just a few items remained.

"Let's close up," Sally whispered. "This place is giving me the creeps. We can give the rest of this stuff to the church rummage sale."

Ann looked around the dreary apartment with its now bare walls showing peeled paint and scuff marks. The last vestige of home, the curtains, still hung on the windows. Purchased by the landlord, they were a sign that soon another hopeful family would be housed in this depressing apartment. Gladly Ann took Sally's suggestion and hurriedly packed an old suitcase with the things she would need for her week's stay at the Canfields.

Not until they were settled in Mrs. Canfield's bright air conditioned kitchen sipping hot coffee and eating homemade sweet rolls, administered by the kind attention of Sally's mother, did Ann's spirits revive.

The money box lay unopened on the table until each had drunk two cups of coffee and consumed a whole pan of hot buttered rolls.

"Shall we?" Ann asked, opening the lid. All three women piled up coins, bills and checks. Agnes Canfield participating as eagerly as Ann and Sally. The grand total came to nine hundred and thirty-seven dollars.

"Marvelous!" Ann said, with genuine pleasure. "I never thought we'd do this well. This, plus my salary, the two hundred from Honest Freddie and the six hundred from my retirement account will give me two thousand three hundred and thirty-seven dollars. Plenty to last until February when the first interest on my bonds comes due. If I can live on three hundred a month, I'll even have an extra five hundred for the built in storage space I need."

As three hundred a month seemed like a pittance

to Sally and her mother, they graciously remained silent, allowing Ann to bask happily in her relative wealth.

Each night that week Sally and Ann returned from work to enjoy a home cooked dinner prepared by the talented hands of Agnes Canfield. This was a new luxury for Ann and she thoroughly enjoyed it, as well as the charming comfort of their home.

Evenings were spent shopping for Sally's career wardrobe. Ann would have been embarrassed going into such expensive shops dressed as she was in second hand maternity clothes if Sally's pleasure hadn't been so contagious. Selecting several tailored dresses at fantastic prices and three suits, even more costly, Sally eagerly charged them on her Master Card. Then serious decisions had to be made as to accessories. Which eighty-five dollar shoes did Ann think would be best with the cream colored suit? Should she buy the matching coat to the green suit, awfully light weight, but so chic an outfit? Ann dreaded to think of Sally's total bill but consoled herself with the thought that the suits, because of color selection, were interchangeable, adding additional outfits to Sally's wardrobe.

When the day came to leave for Northern Wisconsin, Ann's car was bursting. A pedal sewing machine Mrs. Canfield had found in the attic, a box of canning jars found in the same location and an old upright Underwood typewriter Sally had talked Mr. Appleby into giving Ann with the reasoning that, "Maybe you can earn a few pence typing letters," were all jammed in with Ann's own possessions.

Ann bid Agnes Canfield goodby, thanking her for all her kindness. Here is a truly caring mother, Ann thought. I hope I'll be as good a mother.

Sally and Ann walked slowly to the waiting car. Standing by the readied bug, the two friends were unable to speak. Large drops fell from Sally's eyes, a steady stream of tears flowed from Ann's.

"We're a couple of ninnies," Ann said.

"Sure. I'll see you soon, on my first trip to Duluth," Sally answered, wiping her eyes.

"Bring a sleeping bag."

"And a splitting axe too, I suppose," Sally retorted, as Ann squeezed behind the steering wheel.

Chapter 6

Ann drove her loaded car onto her very own property! Opening the solid oak house door, she stood for a moment surveying her domain. The late afternoon sun was still shining in the front window sending welcoming rays of light over the polished hardwood floor. The scene from her east window, now in the shade of a still August day, seemed like a woodland painting. Her possessions, that Jimmy Burns had so kindly driven up, were piled neatly in one corner. Resting beside them were the three mattresses she had ordered. Overcome by the joy of arrival, Ann whispered, "Thank you God for this lovely home and for keeping us in your protective hands."

Deciding to have a relaxing cup of coffee before unpacking, Ann opened the chimney flue and went out the back door to collect dried twigs for a fire. A few feet from the house, neatly stacked in long rows at least four feet high, was a huge collection of firewood. Unbelieving, Ann walked around the cords of wood three times. Must be enough for the whole year, she thought in amazement. Oh, how good and kind everyone was in this tiny village. Now all her fears of not being able to secure enough wood for the winter were laid to rest. Her babies would be snug and warm no matter how severe the weather.

Starting a fire, Ann waited to see that it was burning well. Assured, she put on the tea kettle and realizing it would be some time before the stove heated up enough to boil water, took her extra milk, butter and eggs, secure in a tightly covered pail, to the creek. Here she lowered the pail onto the rocky bottom and as an extra precaution tied the pail handle to a nearby tree. Tomorrow morning will tell, she thought, returning to the cabin.

Not having kerosene lamps, as yet, Ann put one three inch candle in the middle of the table and a regular sized one in its pewter holder on top of her boxed possessions. Keeping the fire going, she cooked a simple hamburger dinner and pleased with her ability to provide a meal from a wood stove, ate it with relish. Now refreshed, she unpacked the car, placing items on the floor where she hoped to store them later in proper cupboards. Then making up one of her beds she put it under her favorite window, changed to a night gown and was soon fast asleep, well before the setting sun required the use of the carefully placed candles.

The morning rays coming through the east window,

woke Ann from a deep sleep. She lay quietly, surveying her home with pleasure. Then aware of all that must be accomplished before the babies arrived, rose and dressed.

It was a lovely summer day, bright and clear, the temperature in the low seventies this early in the morning. Ann sauntered along the road toward her aunt's home enjoying the smell of newly cut hay, whiffs of pine, the sound of singing birds and the sight of deer tracks in the sandy road.

She was greeted by her delighted aunt and uncle; Albert, anxious to see her plans for building in storage space and Eva, equally anxious to hear how her first pioneer experience had gone.

With pride she told them of her ability to obtain water, keep her milk and eggs cool and cook on a wood stove.

"But who cut all that marvelous firewood and piled it so neatly by the cabin?" Ann asked. "That is one of the most precious gifts I have ever received."

Uncle Albert laughed, delighted with her response. "Actually, I took a little liberty with your land," he began. "Albert Gunther, who lives in the house next to the church, that ram shackled affair with all those cars out front, asked if he could cut firewood on your land. I knew there was plenty of dead wood for both of you and as he is an honest, hardworking man, I said he could if he would cut enough for you as well. We left it that he would pile up your wood this year as I knew you wouldn't have time. But after this he'll just saw it up and dump it by the back door; you'll have to do the stacking. That is, if you agree to the arrangement for future years."

"Agree! Sent from heaven. I don't think I'll ever be

able to saw up enough wood for an entire winter."

"Oh, he's an old logging man, has a power saw and does the whole thing in a week or so. You may have to split some of those logs, but you can do that as you use the wood. Splits easier in cold weather anyway."

"But, however do I pay him for stacking all the wood?" Ann questioned, concerned about taking on a debt obligation.

"He had help," Aunt Eva interjected, knowing Albert tired when conversation became extended. "Winthrop Jacobson, the gray haired man with the beard, who sat next to Alice Ruffles at the church dinner. You'll get to know them all in time," Aunt Eva reassured her, when Ann looked puzzled. "He lives in the house next to Abner Gunther, coming this way. Place with all the flowers out front. He and his wife have green thumbs. Anyway, you can just give them both some apples, come fall. You have the only good trees in the village. Must be because yours are protected by the barn. Most apple trees don't do well up here, probably because the winters are too cold."

Apples, Ann thought, I've already promised the fruit from two trees to Seth Ruffles. My goodness, everyone up here seems to live on a barter system. My apples are as good as gold. I just hope I have some left after I pay all my debts.

"Now let's just look at those plans of yours," Uncle Albert suggested.

They spent the next hour discussing Ann's shelving arrangements; changing a few, adding open shelves on the right side of the desk and hanging holders for cooking pans above the counter top giving Ann more shelf space in the kitchen area for such items as salt, yeast and spices. Satisfied, Uncle Albert started dictating the lumber order to Aunt Eva, while Ann, pails in hand, left to pick blackberries.

She would be picking for Mrs. Jones, the seventy year old lady in the two story yellow house as well as for the Gilberts and herself. A reassuring thought, for soon she would be ahead, at least with one of her neighbors. It was also nice to know that her first attempts at jelly making would be under the watchful eye of Aunt Eva.

Stopping at her rural mail box, Ann was surprised to find a letter. The California return address gave her a hint as to the sender. During her lunch of milk and an egg salad sandwich she read Roger's message.

> Blackberries along creek edge.
> I dream of homemade blackberry jelly.
>   Roger Anderson

The nerve of him, she thought, hinting I send him some jelly. Besides I know the berries are down by the creek. That is one of the first things Seth Ruffles mentioned when he was showing me the land. Crunching his letter into a ball, Ann threw it in the fire box, ready for burning when she lit the night fire.

Wisely Ann put on a long sleeved shirt, sunglasses and a babushka over her hair. Looking like a Russian peasant, she headed for an afternoon of berry picking. In spite of the thorns which resulted in numerous hand scratches, she experienced a quiet pleasure in filling the pails with the luscious black fruit. Tiring part way through, she placed the half filled pails carefully on mounds of grass, took off her shoes and cooled her legs in the crystal clear creek that flowed beside the bushes. Tiny fish swam around her feet, a blue jay stopped for a drink and two gray squirrels raced around the trunk of a tree, unconcerned with her presence. Further down the stream, a doe, tense with alertness, ears forward to pick up any unnatural sound, stood above the stream. Ann remained still, hardly breathing. The graceful head bent to the water, drank, then with one motion, the doe turned and bounded into the forest. I'm living in paradise, Ann decided, deeply content.

After the pails were filled, her hands dipped in the refreshing water to clean the numerous scratches, Ann leisurely walked home. Coming around the barn, she anxiously inspected her apple trees or gold mine as she had come to think of the fruit laden branches. The apples were nearing full size, but were still a hard green color. Unaware as to anything she should be doing for their care and not even knowledgeable enough to know when they would be ripe, she just suggested, "Keep growing, I need you."

Following a rest in the shade of the backyard Oak tree, Ann divided the berries and headed for the yellow house with Mrs. Jones' portion. Her pace was leisurely; there was no need to hurry for she and Aunt Eva wouldn't be making jelly until the following morning. As there was no front walk, Ann found herself crossing a recently mowed lawn to a green front door guarded by two large pots of geraniums. Mrs. Jones, a gray haired, tall, thin woman opened the door before Ann could knock.

Mindful of Mrs. Jones' seventy plus years, Ann felt immediately protective. "I'll carry this in the kitchen for you."

"Never mind," Mrs. Jones answered, easily picking up the two gallon pail and marching off to the kitchen. Placing the berries on the table, she viewed them with a frown. "They cook down quite a bit, you know," she said pointedly.

Rather surprised, Ann replied, "I thought two gallons would be plenty for one person. You do live alone, don't you?"

"Have for the last twenty years," Mrs. Jones proudly proclaimed. "Ever since my husband died. But I like some extra jelly for gifts. You don't suppose tomorrow—-?" Mrs. Jones shifted into a voice that reminded Ann of her fifth grade teacher, the ability to make a request, a command.

"I'll be picking again tomorrow afternoon," Ann said. "How much would you like?"

"A bushel." Mrs. Jones pressed her advantage.

"A bushel!" Ann exclaimed, shocked by the amount. She hadn't picked a bushel for all three families. "You wouldn't, by any chance, be planning on using jelly for a payment system, would you?"

Mrs. Jones blushed, a red that started at her neck and crept slowly across her face. "Well, make it two more gallons. That should do," she stammered, avoiding Ann's question. Which didn't matter as Ann already knew the answer.

Glancing around the cluttered room, Ann noticed piles of material in one corner, the top pieces no larger than an inch wide, plants of all shapes and sizes growing or attempting to grow by the window and a refrigerator covered with small ugly felt note holders. No sooner had her eyes rested on the magnetic holders when Mrs. Jones plucked one, in the vague form of a butterfly with two sequins on the tips of each wing and handed it to Ann.

"For being so nice to pick blackberries for me," she

said with what she considered a gracious smile.

"Thank you," Ann said weakly.

"Would you like some tea?" Mrs. Jones added, extending her hospitality. "I make it from wild flower leaves."

"No, thank you," Ann replied hurriedly, conscious of the fact that she was feeding three, two of whom were too young to deal with strange concoctions. Gradually the realization came to her that retreat would be the wisest move. Hastily she picked up the now empty pails and backed toward the front door.

"I'd better stop in to see my aunt," Ann remarked, as she made her escape.

Clutching her felt butterfly, a sickly purple in color, Ann cut across both lawns to the Gilberts.

No sooner had she stepped inside the kitchen than Aunt Eva noticed the purple felt butterfly. Without visibly pausing in her cabinet cleaning, Aunt Eva reached down and opened a drawer beside the sink. The entire drawer was filled with Mrs. Jones' handiwork: odd shaped teddy bears, blue ducks with sequin eyes and a whole section of black felt in the vague form of squirrels or chipmunks.

Ann looked at Uncle Albert, Aunt Eva looked at Ann, within seconds all three were overcome with hilarious laughter.

"I hope you didn't stay for tea," Aunt Eva said between bouts of mirth.

"I used you for a quick retreat," Ann said, beginning to get herself under control.

"Smart girl," Uncle Albert remarked, his laughter easing to a few chuckles. "And I suppose she wasn't satisfied with what you brought her."

"Oh no, she wanted a bushel."

"Good old Mrs. Jones," Eva said. "She pushes the village to the limit. Has ever since Mr. Jones died and that was twenty years ago. I'll never forget the time Abner washed all her windows and she gave him a felt teddy bear. He was fit to be tied. Especially as everyone knows her husband worked for the railroad and she gets a nice pension. Now we all take care of her, sort of spread it around. Everyone in the village must have a drawer full of these."

"You mean I'm just starting my collection?" Ann asked in horror.

Her aunt and uncle just smiled; they were too weak to start laughing again.

"What will she do with all that jelly?" Ann asked, knowing Mrs. Jones could whip up a felt do-dad in seconds and must have an endless supply.

"Saves the jelly for the kids. They're too smart to work for her unless they know before hand what the reward will be," Aunt Eva answered in a tone that indicated she sometimes wondered why the community didn't follow the leadership of the children.

"You just forget about picking more berries for her," Uncle Albert remarked with fatherly concern. "We said we take care of Mrs. Jones, but we don't let her push us around. What you gave her was enough for her needs."

"Are you sure that would be all right? I mean I would like to spend my time getting a good supply for us."

"Of course it would be all right. Eva will call and tell her that today's supply is all we can give her."

"She is quite reasonable when you put your foot down," Aunt Eva added, "Besides May Gunther is planning on doing a lot of picking this year. I'm sure

May will give Mrs. Jones a bucket or two."

The following morning Ann took her cleaned berries to the Gilberts. Together she and Aunt Eva strained the blackberries and with sugar and pectin added, put a large kettle on to reach a rapid boil. Depositing paraffin wax in an old coffee can, Aunt Eva set this to melt in a pan of hot water.

"Makes it nice, using an old can, you can just leave the extra wax in the can for the next batch of jelly," she instructed.

Putting Ann to work scouring old mayonnaise jars, former pickle containers or used peanut butter jars, Aunt Eva supervised the bubbling fruit. Satisfied that all was cooked to perfection, Eva skimmed off the foam and allowed Ann to fill the sterilized jars, leaving a half inch space at the top. Taking charge again, Aunt Eva eased about an eighth of an inch of hot paraffin over each container. Setting their handiwork aside to cool, they rewarded themselves with cups of coffee. Between them they had eight jars of smooth jelly with labels that read, "Blackberry 1979."

"How many more shall we do?" Ann asked, constantly glancing at the cooling jars, inordinately proud of her contribution.

"Best to do extra," Aunt Eva answered. "This is a good year for blackberries, some years the crop is mighty poor.

As Ann's lumber for the cabinets and shelves wouldn't arrive until the following Monday, she was quite confident she would have this entire week to devote to jelly making. Being unaware of country ways, she was unprepared for the surprise that awaited her at home.

Chapter 7

Proudly carrying her precious cargo of four jars of jelly, Ann walked the mile to her home, mentally planning her lunch from the meagre food supply she had brought from Hampton. Walking up the drive she noticed several paper bags resting against her front door. Investigation found them to contain string beans, cucumbers and zucchini, an enormous amount of each. There was no note or any other indication as to the donor or donors.

"How amazing!" Ann voiced her wonder, unable to believe what she was seeing. Putting her prize jars of jelly on the kitchen counter, Ann returned to the front doorway and re-examined her gifts. One whole bag of string beans, a bag of zucchini and half a bag of cucumbers.

"What lovely, lovely people live in Pinewood," Ann said aloud, still unable to believe that so many people were concerned for her welfare.

She carried the bags of vegetables inside and put them on the table. Over a quick lunch of sliced cucumbers, bread, butter and blackberries in milk, Ann reluctantly abandoned plans for an afternoon of berry picking. There was no choice but to begin canning vegetables, her mysterious supply was much too large for her to consume fresh. This meant lighting the fire in the hottest part of the day and figuring out the mysteries of a pressure cooker, for Aunt Eva was emphatic that all vegetables must be pressure sealed.

Carefully reading the directions that came with the cooker, several times, Ann began the process of canning beans. The string beans had to be washed and cut, the jars and lids sterilized and the water brought to the correct temperature. It was long after dinner time - Ann having opened her precious tuna fish to expedite this meal - before a hot, tired homemaker was able to ease herself into a kitchen chair and gaze lovingly at ten quarts of string beans and twelve quarts of zucchini, cooling on the brick section of the floor, with only a bag of cucumbers yet to be processed.

Too exhausted to consider the cucumbers, Ann washed her face and hands in cold water and prepared for bed. The still hot wood stove radiated oppressive heat. Her only recourse was to leave the casement windows open as far as possible and the back door ajar with the screen hooked, hoping the evening air would soon make sleeping possible.

Why was I concerned about not having a radio or a

television, she thought, gratefully easing her tired body onto the bed. There isn't a drop of time left for television. The smile, this idea brought to her face, was still there when she fell asleep.

Sunrise found her eating oatmeal while her bath water heated, an unusually early start for she was determined to make pickle relish in the coolness of the morning. Selecting a recipe that promised to be sweet enough for her taste, Ann found that the cucumbers needed to be salted and left to stand overnight and that she lacked green peppers and cider vinegar. Thwarted in her attempts to make relish until the following day, Ann cut up and salted the cucumbers, then happily set out to pick blackberries, feeling that she had just been let out of school for a holiday and only hoping the village store, which she would have to visit later, carried cider vinegar.

Berries duly picked, Ann dropped them off at the cottage and leisurely walked down her dirt road toward town and the village store. Last night's fresh deer tracks accompanied her part way; she could recognize the prints of a large buck and two doe. My new neighbors, she thought contentedly.

The village store, consisting as it did of restaurant, gas station and grocery supplier could hardly be evaluated from the front entrance, so crowded was it with six foot high isles crammed with supplies. Just at one end, where three checkered cloth tables were jammed together, was there any overhead space. Two truck drivers were seated at one table, drinking coffee and eating homemade sweet rolls, for which Holly Fines was famous. This fame causing many a traveling man to stop for refreshments in spite of the unpleasantly crowded conditions.

The grocery section consisted of basic staples, a large display of snack foods and assorted soft drinks and, against one wall, a refrigerator section for milk, butter, margarine and eggs. Unable to find cider vinegar, Ann took a gallon of milk and found her way to the cash register.

"You're Ann Randall, aren't you?" Holly Fines asked cheerfully. "Bought Roger Anderson's log cabin, I hear."

"Yes," Ann agreed, immediately liking this pleasant appearing woman with her broad open smile.

"Anything else I can get you?"

"I did want some cider vinegar for making pickle relish, but I don't see any."

"Oh, I keep it out back," Holly said. Going out a side door she returned shortly with a half gallon jug. "We always try to keep the village needs in mind. This time of year it's lots of vinegar, sugar and canning jars."

Holly's Scandinavian blue eyes sparkled as she placed the jug of vinegar on the counter top. "You care to order up for the winter? Helps a lot to have a good supply when the snow flies."

"What do you mean?" Ann asked, intrigued.

"Well, Ben and I take orders for things like flour and sugar in hundred or fifty pound sacks. Come the end of September he'll make a trip to the cities, get everyone's order and set them up real nice for the winter."

"How marvelous," Ann said, envisioning her plastic barrels, which she had yet to purchase, filled to the brim with oatmeal, flour, wheat flour and sugar. Placing her order, Ann felt well satisfied with her day's accomplishments.

"Thanks for all your help," she said when their business transactions were complete.

"Oh, glad to do what I can. Anything special you need, just ask and we'll try and get it for you," Holly said, seeing her newest customer to the door. "When fall comes I'll see you at the church quilt making sessions. Our business eases off by then giving me time to do a little visiting with friends and help at the church."

Again Ann found her evening absorbed with canning gift vegetables and the following morning consumed with making pickle relish. Not until afternoon was she able to take the latest batch of blackberries to the Gilberts for jelly making. Their second batch of jelly processed, Aunt Eva, Uncle Albert and Ann took time to rest in the yard under the shade of two maple trees. Ann took off her sneakers and wiggled her toes in the warm grass. The iced tea they had brought from the house cooled and refreshed their heated bodies. Bluejays, gold finches and an occasional nuthatch flew leisurely from Aunt Eva's bird feeder to nearby trees and back again, when hunger required. Ann closed her eyes to rest from the day's labors and to allow herself to absorb the peace of the country. She could hear the faint rustling of wind moved leaves and the chirping of birds. The smell of hay mixed with the sweet aroma of lilies drifted in the air.

"Don't get discouraged," Aunt Eva said, directing her remark to her niece. "This is the busy time of year for country folk. We all work twenty hours a day during harvest time, but we get our reward come winter when we can sit by a cozy, warm fire and open jars of homemade goodies."

Uncle Albert sipped his iced tea from a straw anchored in a covered mug. "The September crops are a little easier to care for," he said, adding to the reassurance. "Potatoes and winter squash you just store in the root cellar. Even carrots and your apples will last quite a time there. Though it is best to can both the carrots and the apples you expect to last through the entire winter."

"That is good news!" Ann exclaimed. "My first garden may be ninety percent potatoes and winter squash," she joked, knowing their attempts at encouragement came because she had told them of her hours of effort canning string beans and zucchini and making pickle relish.

Thinking again of the proud display of homemade jelly cooling in Aunt Eva's kitchen, Ann added, "Did I tell you, Roger Anderson sent me a note hinting that I send him some blackberry jelly?"

To Ann's surprise, Aunt Eva was sympathetic. "Oh, that poor boy. I suppose he misses his home. Must be awfully different out there in California."

"Poor boy! He must be making a fortune writing for television."

Ignoring Ann's remark, Aunt Eva went on in a casual voice, "His mother isn't able to make jelly anymore, her eye sight has been failing for the past few years." Pouring each of them more tea, she added, "She sends him a box of goodies once a month."

"Why don't we give Alma Anderson a jar of jelly?" Ann suggested, trying to get away from the subject of Roger Anderson.

"Oh, Alice Ruffles does that. In fact, Alice is over at Alma Anderson's right now, helping her pack Roger's box." This time Ann got a direct, purposeful look.

"All right, I'm getting the hint," Ann said laughing. "I'll take a jar over to Mrs. Anderson, the smallest one. Only I reserve the right to add to the label."

"What are you going to add?" Aunt Eva questioned, her brows coming together in a definite frown.

"Under protest," Ann quipped.

Uncle Albert, who had remained silent during their exchange, now burst into laughter. Aunt Eva ignored both of them, pretending to be busy examining her flower garden.

It wasn't until Ann was half way to Mrs. Anderson's, a neat white bungalow directly across from the church, that it dawned on her there might be a village conspiracy. They wouldn't be trying to match Roger and me, would they, she wondered. Surely not, Ann decided, easing her bulging frame up the newly scrubbed front steps.

Beaming at Ann with the sweetest of smiles, Alma Anderson took Ann's hand and lead her into a sparkling pink and white kitchen.

"I'm so glad you've come. I have so wanted to welcome you to our village, but my eyes, you know. Very hard for me to walk on unpaved roads. I can't tell you how happy we are that you have decided to settle here. Your coming has cheered Albert and Eva ever so much."

Such praise and such obvious sincerity from this white haired, pink cheeked woman sent Ann scurrying to cover her caustic words on the jelly label. Fortunately Alice Ruffles was packing the famous, Hollywood bound box. Easing the blackberry jelly into Alice's hands, Ann suggested a likely spot in one corner. Maddeningly, Alice held up the jar, admiring its rich color. Having lost control, Ann could only carry on a conversation with Alma, hoping to distract her from also admiring Roger's latest gift. Minutes seemed to pass before Alice finally wrapped the glass jar in a protective towel, placed it in the box and sealed the contents.

"Ann and I will see this gets off right away, Alma," Alice said, taking charge. Refusing refreshments she ushered Ann out the door with promises to visit longer next time.

Turning at the end of the walk, Ann saw Alma Anderson, still with a smile, waving a cheerful goodby, her white hair framed by the deep blue flowers of a Climatis that arched over her spotlessly clean front porch.

"What a sweet lady," Ann remarked.

"Under protest," Alice quoted, a smile finally breaking forth on her rugged, leathery face.

"Well, he practically asked for the jelly!" Ann defended her label, with a tone of voice that expressed her annoyance. "Besides, I didn't know his mother was so nice," she added, beginning to feel a bit ashamed of her reaction to Roger.

"Actually, Roger is rather nice also. He keeps Alma's house painted and in good repair and pays for her three months in Florida during the winter. Of course, right now he is a bit overcome with his own importance, but that will pass." Positive that she had explained Roger, Alice went on quickly, "What I really wanted to tell you is that there will be a farm auction on Friday, about ten miles out of town, at the old Burnum place. I'm going and I hope you will go with me. Eva said you still need kerosene lamps and some gardening tools. You could pick up some good buys there."

"Why, I would love to. That is if I'm not overwhelmed by silent vegetable donations."

"Stack them up, they can wait a day," Alice

instructed. "You wouldn't mind taking a turn at the food booth while we are at the auction, would you? The church ladies sell hot dogs, pop, coffee and cake at all auctions. Great way to raise money for the church."

"I'll be glad to," Ann agreed.

"Good, I'll put you down to work with Phyllis Westland from eleven to one. Hope neither one of you has to leave for the maternity ward until after the auction."

Having settled all business, Alice Ruffles left to take care of the mailing chores, leaving Ann with the impression that she had just encountered the chairperson of the entire village. Impressed with such efficiency Ann tackled her waiting vegetables without hesitation, finishing another round of canning before the stimulus of Alice Ruffles had worn off.

The next day Ann drove to Hendersonville, the nearest large town, some ten miles from Pinewood. She had a doctor's appointment and plans for purchasing cloth to make diapers and baby clothes. As no car left Pinewood without three or four additional shopping lists, Ann found herself also struggling with Mrs. Jones' sloppy writing, Aunt Eva's penance for abbreviation and Alma Anderson's extremely neat, but minute lettering. It was well into the afternoon before she deciphered and purchased all required items, including her material to make diapers, which she fortunately found on sale. An added blessing on the day was that there were no garden produce awaiting her return and she was able to spend a leisurely evening, strolling around her property, admiring the ripening apples, budding golden rod, the evening flight of barn swallows feasting on the wing and the melodious songs of birds settling down for the night. By the light of an evening candle, Ann wrote a lengthy letter to Sally Canfield.

Punctually, at the stroke of 9:00 a.m. on Friday, Alice Ruffles called for Ann in her Chevy pick-up.

"I brought the truck in case either one of us buys something too large for the car. You can never tell with an auction. You may come home with something you never dreamed of owning."

"What happens? Do you get carried away with the bidding?" Ann asked, finding it hard to imagine Alice Ruffles loosing control in any situation.

"Well, yes, and the wonderful prices and the general festive atmosphere. It's really quite a party." Alice gave Ann a quick knowing smile, before returning her gaze to the road.

That smile told Ann they were riding in the truck for Ann's convenience or in case she lost control under the influence of the auctioneer's hypnotic jargon.

The rest of the ten mile drive to the Burnum auction was taken up with Alice giving instructions on how best to manage the food booth.

When they were within a half mile of the farm, Ann could see cars and trucks parked all along both shoulders of the road, an unbelievable number as if every person within a hundred mile radius was at the auction. Alice drove right through this hedge of motor vehicles and onto the Burnum front lawn, presumedly the parking lot for those with special privileges.

Numerous families were wandering happily among the house furnishings, displayed in the back yard and walking well worn paths to the barn and out buildings to view farm machinery and other paraphernalia waiting for the auction block. The temperature was already eighty degrees on a cloudless August morning.

Wise folks, knowing this was an all day event, had already set up lawn chairs under fifty year old oaks scattered about the farm.

Alice disappeared immediately to help with the auction, allowing Ann the freedom to leisurely wander about inspecting garden tools, household items and the genuinely joyous atmosphere. Reverend and Sara Woodbind stopped to say hello and recommend she bid on a sturdy garden shovel. Abner Gunther paused briefly to grumble about the high prices the auctioneer was getting for the larger farm machinery and to warn her to beware of antique dealers who would pay outrageous prices for some items.

Behind the farm house was a long row of stacked kitchen ware. Here Ann found a hand operated washing machine, made of wood with a metal interior and wooden agitating handle. About half the size of a modern machine, it would accommodate small loads and to Ann's thinking, perfect for diaper washing. Placed by her bath tub it could easily drain into the tub, if a small hose was attached to the bottom drain opening.

"Ann, that would be perfect for you," Phyllis Westland said, coming up to inspect the washer.

"That is exactly what I thought," Ann agreed.

"You must bid on it," Phyllis added. "But do come have a cup of coffee with me. They won't get to the women's stuff until afternoon. We have plenty of time. They always start with farm machinery and barn equipment, which takes hours to auction off."

Coffee in hand, Ann and Phyllis sat in the Westland's lawn chairs in the cool shade of one of the oaks, within view of the entire proceedings.

"This is old hat for Jim and me," Phyllis explained.

"We have learned how to be comfortable at these affairs. Half our farm came through the auction block."

Off at a distance they could see a large group of jean clad men crowded around a farm wagon on which the auctioneer, pointer in hand, bellowed out instructions. "Who'll bid 25 - 25?" drifted above the chatter of children and the call of neighbor to neighbor.

"I'm glad you're working with me at the chuck wagon," Phyllis said.

"So am I," Ann agreed. "But I think Alice was a little nervous putting us together."

"With Alice Ruffles in charge, these babies wouldn't dare come today," Phyllis said laughing. "As town organizer, she would never forgive them."

"I got the same impression," Ann said, joining in the laughter. When they could control themselves, Ann asked, "Phyllis, have you been leaving all those wonderful vegetables at my door?"

"No. They must be from the town gardeners. Everyone is too busy at harvest time for visits, so they just drop off gifts and run. Come winter they will stop by for a nice chat and ask how you liked the beans or cucumbers or whatever. Best to have lots of coffee and cakes or cookies on hand, come November."

"Oh, that's how it works! What a relief to know that come fall I'll know who to thank."

"By the way, I've been meaning to bring you some eggs. I know you won't want to start your own flock until spring," Phyllis said, reaching into a picnic basket to offer Ann a piece of banana bread.

"Thanks," Ann said, accepting the banana bread and a second cup of coffee. "Fresh eggs from your farm would be nice. But do you think I could raise chickens? I could fence off the end of the old barn for a chicken house but what do I feed them, how do I take care for them and where would I get the birds?"

"Of course you could manage a few hens. Women have been raising chickens for generations. I'll tell you all about it when you're ready and I can sell you a few hens and a rooster or two to get started. I do have a good flock of Rhode Island Reds," Phyllis replied.

"Perfect, I'll plan that for my first spring project."

"Are you doing all right for money? I don't want to be nosy but the Gilberts say you are on a tight budget."

"I'm not sure, with all the extra expenses of getting started I've spent more than I planned. It would be nice to pick up some extra money doing typing," Ann said thoughtfully. "I can turn out a very professional business letter."

"Good, I'll pass the word around. In fact, my Jim may be over to use your talents; he gets raving now and then over some government farm policy or bureaucratic tom foolery, as he puts it."

"Thanks, Phyllis, I really appreciate your help. Everyone in Pinewood has been so kind and helpful. I keep thanking the Lord for this Christian community."

"I only wish you'd moved here three years ago so Roger would have met you before he moved to California."

"Roger Anderson, the successful Hollywood writer? The man my aunt raves about as an ideal son and village hero?"

"Oh, he's still a devoted son and model of success to the older generation," Phyllis admitted. "But believe me, he isn't the same all around great guy that he used to be. I didn't see him the last time he was home, before he flew to Hawaii, but I saw him the time before. He came out to our house with his latest lady friend.

When I think of her I see bleached hair, a tight skirt and restless hands moving numerous rings around fingers with green painted fingernails. Her topics of conversation were expensive cars, jewelry and parties. The sad part about it was, I think Roger was seriously interested in her. How he could be, I haven't the faintest idea, but he seemed to be intrigued."

"Was she pretty?" Ann asked.

"Yes, in a flashy way. But Roger is quite good looking in a dark, very masculine way. He has tight muscle, slim hips and broad shoulders, the kind of build you see on swimmers and tennis players and he's good at both sports. Women are attracted to Roger. Unfortunately he may be lost in the glitter and glamour of money and look down on country home town values."

"I don't think I'd like him from what I've heard. He sounds so impressed with his own importance. Can you imagine telling someone you're glad they can't afford to modernize their home and in the next letter asking for jelly?"

"He asked for homemade jelly! That's encouraging." Phyllis said, beginning to smile. Ann couldn't figure out why, so let it pass.

Business at the chuck wagon was brisk between eleven and one o'clock. Alice, Phyllis and Ann served scores of hot dogs, gallons of coffee, in spite of the heat and uncountable cans of soft drinks and candy bars. Each purchaser had a tale to tell of unheard of bargains they had obtained by out bidding their neighbors or the strangers who had driven in from the Twin Cities.

Ann was able to obtain the washing machine for the marvelous sum of five dollars, as well as a hoe, a spade and a rake. There was competition for the garden tools, but Ann had a feeling it was half hearted, her Pinewood friends quickly dropping out once she entered the bidding. She did have to forgo a kerosene lamp, for an antique dealer bid it up beyond her means.

Joyously Ann carried home her new treasures. While Alice, pleased with the churches profits on the luncheon sales and the fact that neither of her pregnant workers had deserted, eagerly talked of her next plans for raising missionary monies.

Chapter 8

The lumber arrived on the last Monday in August. On Tuesday, Uncle Albert was so excited he convinced Seth to transport his wheel chair and himself the mile down the dirt road, in order to supervise the construction. Seth Ruffles and Abner Gunther would be putting up the frame work, leaving only the shelving for Ann to secure in place. Both men had agreed to take a day out of their busy fall schedules in return for a home cooked meal, if Mrs. Gunther and the two Gunther teenagers could be included. With her aunt and uncle joining them this meant a meal for eight. Nervous over such an important dinner, Ann baked a carrot cake the night before and consulted Phyllis regarding the main course. Fortunately Phyllis had some nice fat broilers ready for plucking and Ann was able to provide roast chicken, mashed potatoes, gravy and a squash casserole.

With the two teenage Gunthers pressed into service, the log cabin resounded with the pounding of nails, the groans of men holding heavy boards, the shouts of, "A little more this way," and above it all the commands of Uncle Albert.

This is like a barn raising, Ann thought, going from checking her cooking dinner to screwing in shelf braces. Even Aunt Eva and May Gunther joined in the construction so by the time they all sat down for dinner, the formica counter top was in place, shelves were secure on the kitchen wall and Ann's preserve area was waiting for the proud display of her jellies, canned string beans, zucchini, four precious jars of sweet corn and the pickle relish.

The doors on her clothing cabinets were not in place, but the bars and shelves were. In the morning she would be able to unpack and arrange all her clothing, blankets and linen. A thought that helped her through the evening of an exhausting but exhilarating day. It was ten o'clock at night before her group of proud workers went home. Seth promising to return the next evening to finish her desk, which he insisted required his expert construction ability.

No sooner had they left then Ann fell into bed, completely happy, but terribly tired. She overslept the next morning and didn't arise until nine-thirty. Yesterday had been a harder day than she thought. Wearily she placed her small wardrobe in the designated closet and made a beef stew for Seth Ruffle's dinner.

Her actions were so slow that that was all she

accomplished before Seth arrived. They sat down to a silent dinner, which Ann could hardly eat. She had just washed up the dishes, while Seth was putting the desk top in place, when she felt a sudden contraction. In a few minutes there was another one. Holding her mouth, so she wouldn't cry out, Ann sat heavily on a kitchen chair. The pains continued at set intervals, a sharp one causing her to cry out even with her mouth covered.

Instantly alert, Seth asked, "What's the matter?" His old ugly face showed alarm, somehow making his crooked nose even more prominent.

"You'll have to drive me to the hospital, I think the babies are coming," Ann said, all in one breath.

"Oh, no, not me, woman!" Seth implored, his leathery face turning chalk white.

"You'll have to!" she insisted, walking to the door between contractions, picking up a small readied suitcase on the way.

Not until Ann had somehow gained a seat in Seth's old battered truck did he, resigned to the inevitable, climb in the driver's seat. Throwing the truck into reverse, he just missed an oak tree before shifting to low and heading down the road in a sudden, grinding burst of speed. Gripping the steering wheel with both massive, hard worked hands, he pressed his foot to the floor. They shot down the highway toward Hendersonville, the truck at its maximum speed of forty miles an hour. Which to Ann, with all the rattles and bumps, seemed like eighty.

"You don't have to rush, the first baby takes hours," she said, clenching her teeth.

"Says you!" Seth muttered, now weaving back and forth down the highway. She looked to see tears streaming down his still white cheeks. Astonished to see the condition this strong, brave man was in, Ann could only pray they would arrive in one piece.

The pressed old truck began to sputter, backfiring now and then as they continued to weave back and forth across the road. Arriving in Hendersonville, unmindful of the increased traffic, Seth pressed on, shooting down side streets and crossing in front of honking cars, forced to slam on their brakes or face dented fenders.

"Seth, I'm never, ever going to ride with you again!" Ann yelled over the noisy motor. She was so shocked by his driving that she was hardly aware of her increasing pain.

"Fine with me," he yelled back. "I never invited you in the first place."

Miraculously they arrived at the emergency entrance without being killed.

"I'll go my myself," Ann insisted, forcing herself to make it to the hospital door. Mercifully, expert hands took charge and after six hours of pain and struggle, Ann gave birth to two healthy baby girls.

"Rough go," one of the nurses said kindly.

"The ride down was worse," Ann answered.

After a silent, "Thank you," to God for her two darlings, she immediately fell asleep.

For three marvelous, gorgeous days Ann did nothing but eat, sleep and nurse her babies. She reveled in the comfort of being waited on and the opportunity to sleep for hours, only waking long enough in the evening to smile at her visitors and enjoy the excitement the birth of twins was creating in this tiny country hospital.

Refusing to think of the unfinished construction project, the unmade diapers and baby clothes and the fact that she had probably spent well into next months meagre three hundred dollars, Ann marveled at the tiny perfection of each baby and allowed her thoughts to dwell on possible names. One must be Sally, for her dear friend, Sally Canfield and the other Eva, after her supportive Aunt who had no children of her own.

Because she had twins and was nursing, Doctor Durand suggested she stay in the hospital an additional two days. Once reassured that her office insurance would cover the cost, Ann willingly agreed.

At nine o'clock on her fourth night, as Ann was enjoying the luxury of a late night snack, a hospital cart was rolled into her room and Phyllis, groggy with exhaustion, was helped into the other hospital bed.

Smiling weakly, Phyllis muttered, "Don't wake me for a week."

"A boy," the nurse said, enlightening Ann.

"Nine pounds," was barely audible before Phyllis dropped into exhausted sleep.

Much recovered by the next morning, Phyllis ate a hearty breakfast.

"Well, we made it!" she said before biting into her second sweet roll from an extra tray sent up by her mother who worked in the hospital kitchen. "Just think, we've increased the Pinewood population from seventy-one to seventy-four and the winter population from sixty-six to sixty-nine people."

"Least they could do is give us a medal," Ann contributed.

"Let's pass the medals and demand free baby sitting services."

"And let Seth Ruffles take care of my girls! Not on your life!" Ann said in shock.

Phyllis smiled as she brushed back her long blond hair. "Say, I did hear that three different motorists in Hendersonville and one in Pinewood reported Seth to the sheriff's office."

"Good, I hope they put him in jail for a few days. The way he weaved that truck down the road, I was sure the old thing would fall apart right on the highway."

"They did investigate, but once they found out he was driving you to the hospital, the whole force broke into gales of laughter. Seth Ruffles will never live that trip down, poor old soul."

After the babies were brought in, fed and admired amid discussions of schedules and clothing, a large bouquet of beautiful red roses arrived for Ann.

"Wow, gorgeous!" Phyllis exclaimed, admiring their deep velvety texture.

"They're from Sally Canfield," Ann commented, reading the card:

> Congratulations, old shoe. As you can't
> name them both after me – so
> confusing – I'll settle for one new,
> brilliant Sally. Mother making
> christening dresses. We'll both be up.

"Did you name one Sally?" Phyllis asked.

"Oh, yes. Sally is the dearest friend. You'll love her. She has become a career woman, out to make a fortune, but great fun when she is relaxed and out of all those designer clothes."

Their room door opened softly and Phyllis' husband peeked into the room, a soft shy smile on his sun tanned face, the smile of a man used to spending hours alone working the farm. Big boned, as was his wife, his massive muscular hands held a tiny gift wrapped package. Nodding politely to Ann, Jim Westland looked at his wife with such devotion that Ann's heart ached. There was no proud father to hold Ann in his arms, to kiss and praise her. A vivid picture of Tom as he was when they first married crossed her mind, making her sadness almost unbearable.

Thankfully, Alice Ruffles arrived, before Ann's spirits hit rock bottom.

"Well, it's all set," Alice announced confidently. She advanced quickly into the room, her steel rimmed glasses reflected the light pouring in the hospital window, while her tightly curled gray hair remained perfectly in place, unaffected by her swift movements.

"Hello, Jim, and congratulations. Fine healthy boy you've got there. All of nine pounds, I hear. Suppose you've already bought him a football and a baseball."

Jim Westland retreated closer to his wife, mumbling something no one heard.

But Phyllis and Ann, aware of Alice's mania for organization, asked in unison, "What's all set?"

Turning to Ann, Alice said, "Why, Seth is going to drive you and the babies home. He'll be here at four this afternoon."

"No, he isn't! I swore I would never ride with him again," Ann said emphatically, rising from her relaxed position on the bed. The faint sound of quiet giggling seemed to be coming from the other hospital bed, but this Ann ignored.

"Ann, you don't mean that," Alice spoke in her soothing motherly voice. "Seth has spent hours polishing his truck. You can't imagine how proud he is to be involved in all this, twins and everything."

"Polishing his truck! There isn't enough paint on that truck to be polished; it's all rust," Ann retorted disdainfully. However her resolve was weakening for she was now having more difficulty blocking off the laughter emitting from Phyllis and Jim. The laughter grew louder. Unable to ignore their amusement any longer Ann said, "Go ahead laugh, you don't have to ride with him." This comment only increased their mirth.

"You had better notify the sheriff," Jim told Alice, containing himself long enough to speak. "Give him time to warn the other motorists." Turning to his wife he added, "Honey, remind me to stay off the road this afternoon." Sitting on the edge of the bed, his arm around his wife, the two made a perfect picture of blond Nordic healthiness and happy contentment mingled with amusement.

Ignoring Jim's remarks, Alice pursued her goal of pleading her brother's cause, with simple minded intensity. "Ann, Seth will be heart broken if you don't ride with him."

"Oh, all right," Ann gave in, seeing the humor of it all.

At four o'clock the grand procession left the hospital room. Ann in a wheelchair carrying Sally - or was it Eva, still hard for her to tell the twins apart - the other twin being carried by a nurse. As the procession moved past the main desk and out of the hospital, Ann looked for Seth Ruffles. Where is my eager chauffeur, she thought, noticing only the back of a tall, thin, gray haired man dressed in slacks and a sport jacket, standing some twenty feet from the hospital entrance. The man turned and advanced toward the waiting group, a silly grin on his ugly face. Ann couldn't believe her eyes, Seth out of his bib overalls and plaid shirt, hair pressed down, with even a necktie! True, the tie was long out of style, but still for him to consider hunting up such a dressy item must mean that this was really one of the important events in his life.

Ready to forgive all and welcome him with a smile, Ann found herself completely ignored. Seth had only one interest, the baby in the nurse's arms. Taking the child from the nurse, he gently gazed at Sally (or was it Eva?), his silly grin broadening, becoming a look of delight. Without a word he carried the baby, secure in her car seat, to the truck and carefully put her on the seat beside himself. Ann was left to be helped in by the now highly amused nurse.

They drove off in silence, this time Seth being extremely careful to the point where they were moving along the highway at twenty-five miles an hour, passed rapidly by every other car on the road. Every now and then Seth took his eyes briefly from the road and glanced at his precious cargo. He's in another world, Ann thought, aware that the silly grin persisted.

"Seth, you live alone, what are you going to do with all the apples from two trees?" Ann asked, tired of being ignored and hoping to obtain a larger barter supply.

"Why, I pass them out to all the good cooks in the village," he answered matter-of-factly. "I haven't had to cook a Saturday or Sunday dinner in years."

There seemed no way to talk Seth out of such a profitable arrangement, so Ann gave up, lapsing into silence. The babies slept peacefully, unmindful of their great adventure. Ann watched the surrounding country side slowly pass from view. The great expanses of forest green were now dotted with specks of red and gold. Now and then a maple tree, bright red at its tips, as if dipped in red paint, sent her heart racing with the joyous reminder of fall colors. Though only the first week in September, the air was brisk, already a few brown leaves caressed the roadside and the goldenrod in its fine yellow blooming, dominated the uncultivated fields.

The pleasure of seeing her sturdy, secure home once again, sent a happy smile across Ann's face. "We're home girls," she said. The baby in her arms opened her blue eyes for a moment, yawned slowly and went back to sleep.

Hearing the old truck arrive - you couldn't miss with the noise it made - Aunt Eva, Alice, Alma Anderson, May Gunther and even Mrs. Jones came out of the log cabin to greet the new village citizens. Within seconds Aunt Eva had secured her name sake (or so Ann thought) cradling the baby Eva in her arms, cooing away to beat the band. Other grandmotherly hands reached for baby Sally, alas unsuccessfully, for the hands that held Sally had also held work horses and two man saws. The ladies were no match for Seth's powerful grip on the car seat and had to be content with grudging permission for quick peeks.

Inside the log cabin, Uncle Albert waited their arrival along with Abner Gunther, the Jacobsons and Reverend Woodbind and his wife. Here in this tiny village surrounded by acres of virgin land, the addition for two more human beings was a cause for celebration.

Her small home was filled with the aroma of brewing coffee. A large cake decorated with pink frosting sat majestically on the kitchen table, surrounded by plates, napkins and forks. There wasn't a scrap of excess lumber to be seen. All her cabinets and shelves had been finished and now glistened with clear varnish, showing the intricate designs of natural wood. Even her hard won jars of home canning were placed neatly on their appropriate shelves. Tears escaped Ann's eyes and trickled down her cheeks, so overcome was she by this show of loving kindness.

"You are all such dears," she said, giving each a quick kiss.

A bit embarrassed, the group drew back to reveal two cradles on the floor by her sofa. They were magnificent works of art. Nordic carvings in solid oak rimmed each tiny bed. A gentle touch produced silent, rhythmic rocking.

Proudly Alma Anderson handed Ann a card.

"Under Protest" - delicious!
For the girls
Roger Anderson

"They are lovely," Ann said sincerely. In truth they are, she thought, cradles fit for princesses. In my humble abode, striped down to the essentials for living, I now have two priceless infant cradles built to last for generations. What wonderful things for the girls to look upon when they're old enough to be aware of artistic beauty.

"We won't stay long. We know you need to get settled," Alice Ruffles announced, emphasizing the we. "A little cake and coffee for all and we'll be on our way."

Seth settled baby Sally in one of the cradles. "She's the one with the dimple when she smiles," he said authoritatively. Pulling a chair over near the cradle he sat down, seeming to guard the young occupant. Aunt Eva placed her namesake in the other cradle and came over to join the group taking plates of cake and cups of coffee.

Over refreshments, Ann was brought up on the village news. The potato crop would be good this year. The trees, turning early, must mean a cold winter. The acorns were abundant; must mean a snowy winter coming. And the caterpillars' coats were thick which must mean a cold, snowy winter on its way.

After Abner had brought in a night's supply of wood, Aunt Eva had mentioned a casserole was in the warmer oven and Reverend Woodbind had blessed the babies, Alice, true to form, ushered the group out the door.

Ann's days soon fell into a pattern. Reading the Bible while eating breakfast, caring for the babies, cooking, canning and cleaning in the mornings. Early afternoon for visits, late afternoon for her children and evenings to wash clothes, sew and read books.

Not until her bank statement came at the end of the month, was Ann jolted out of her blissful existence.

Chapter 9

"I couldn't have spent that much money," Ann told herself in disbelief as she stared at her end of the month balance. Just a few hundred dollars left in an account that had started in the thousands. Nervously she reviewed the bank statement in hopes that somehow they had made a mistake. Every expense listed was accurate. She just hadn't kept close enough track what with the building expenses and the babies coming.

Slowly a cold chill crept over her, even though her home was nice and warm, the babies sleeping comfortably with just light blankets.

For the first time the reality of her situation became very clear. She had been living in a dream world of beautiful scenery, wonderful friends and a delightful family. A dream world she couldn't afford! There was no way a few hundred dollars and the social security money for the children could carry her to the middle of February when the bond interest was due and even if she could make it to February, she still wouldn't be able to pay all their expenses with her combined income. Her children were going to have the best food and the best warm clothing and the best medical care, even if she had to go back to the city to provide that care. The truth was, she couldn't afford to live here in the northwoods very much longer.

Checking to see that the babies were comfortable and assured they were sleeping, Ann put on a sweater and went outside to pace restlessly around the cabin. The last of the fall leaves, rusty red oaks, were crunchy underfoot. Chickadees flew back and forth, watching her from nearby branches.

How can I give up something I love so much, Ann thought. How can I go back to a dismal apartment and have someone I don't even know, care for my children?

My only hope of staying here is to find work I can do at home. I have to figure out how to earn some money. I can't borrow from anyone. Sally would just try to drag me back to the city which I might have to do anyway. Aunt Eva lives on a pretty tight budget herself and Seth Ruffles would never let me forget it, though he probably has a hoard under his mattress. Besides how could I pay it back?

That night Ann crawled into bed with a splitting headache, having spent all afternoon and evening thinking of and rejecting ways of earning money. The only plan she found practical was to put an ad in the Hendersonville paper advertising a typewriting service.

This she could do and do well but there was no guarantee that enough people would use her services to give her an adequate income.

Her headache persisted though dulled down by morning, it remained to plague her. Not until she spoke to God in her morning prayer time did her aching head ease.

"God, help us to remain living here in this beautiful country. But if that isn't your plan for my life help me to accept your direction and be happy wherever you lead me." Ann sighed, it was hard to actually say the last part of her prayer.

Determinedly Ann went about her daily tasks promising herself that she would remain in Pinewood as long as possible and that she would keep her horrible financial situation a complete secret from her friends and family, until the day came that she would have to leave.

On Sunday morning, the week before Sally and her mother were due to arrive for the christening, Seth Ruffles arrived at Ann's door, dressed in his jacket and tie with his gray hair plastered down with some form of slickem.

"Might as well take the girls to church. Get them used to the place," he said matter-of-factly.

Ann hadn't taken the twins to church the previous Sunday for carrying two babies a mile and a half was now beyond her strength. As yet she hadn't figured out a free means of transportation around the village. Even the mile to Aunt Eva's on Friday was fast becoming an impossible weight problem. But at least she had made all the church quilting sessions, for Phyllis Westland picked up the Randall family on Tuesday mornings.

"Be right with you," Ann said eagerly, grabbing one

of her slack suits and heading for the privacy of the bathroom.

Dressed, the girls snug in handmade bunting suits, the group drove in Seth's old truck to the church. Eyebrows raised at the sight of Seth Ruffles entering the building for the first time in years. But no one dared comment, for he marched down to the front row, baby Sally in his arms, nodding solemnly to the assembled congregation, to all the world the master of the situation.

You might know he'd go to the front pew, Ann thought, trailing behind Seth with baby Eva and just hoping the infants wouldn't start crying in the middle of the sermon.

The oldest Sweeney boy, Will, the one who had missed the school bus three days in one week, was racing around the church pews, followed by his four year old sister, Gretta. Mrs. Burton tried unsuccessfully to quiet the older youngsters while still caring for her smallest grandchild. Her whispered instructions were ignored.

Wilber and Marie Burton had recently inherited their three grandchildren, but as Wilber had a weak heart and Marie was naturally a timid soul, they were overwhelmed by their sudden family. Having raised only one child and that child a girl, the Burtons were unprepared for the added energy a combination of children produces, especially a combination that had received little supervision in the past. Will and Gretta found it very easy and often convenient to disregard their grandmother's directives.

Finally, in exasperation, Alice Ruffles stood up in the front pew and demanded, "Will, sit down, right now, and you too, Gretta!"

Both children, stunned by a voice in authority for years, obeyed.

"They just need a firm hand," Alice commented, sitting beside Ann.

Ann's quick glance at Phyllis, across the aisle, was returned with a wink and a smile. Whether Phyllis was amused at Alice's handling of the Sweeney children or the fact that Ann was flanked by Alice Ruffles on one side and Seth Ruffles on the other, Ann couldn't tell. Blowing a reddened nose, Reverend Woodbind approached the lectern.

Chapter 10

"Heavens, I'm going to spend the week-end in a museum!" Sally Canfield announced, opening the front door and sliding her sleeping bag across the floor.

It was late Friday afternoon. Seth was holding a fussing baby, Sally and Ann was making an apple pie in preparation for Sally's visit, which she expected to take place around eight that evening.

Dropping her rolling pin, Ann rushed to greet her dear friend. With a joyous hug they embraced. "I'm so glad you're here," Ann said, admiring the slim sophisticated woman. Sally was dressed in a tailored, fine wool white dress, red jacket, pumps with heels at least three inches high and over her shoulder carried a red and white striped oversized bag. She has dropped another ten pounds, Ann thought, and looks fantastic!

"Mom and I took off early; we couldn't wait to get here. I hope it's okay, our arriving hours ahead of time," Sally said happily, giving her friend an added hug.

"The earlier the better," Ann replied with a delighted smile. "Oh, and Sally, this is Seth Ruffles, baby Sally's other godparent."

Seth was in his usual patched bib overalls, gray hair messed about, unhampered by the greasy stuff he used on special occasions. His cheek was smeared with something that looked suspiciously like baby food. With baby Sally now gurgling happily on his shoulder, he looked critically at the new arrival. Fixing his gaze on her red pumps he spoke thoughtfully, "You wouldn't be much good in the fields."

Sally put down her red and white purse and returned his gaze. "You have one of the ugliest faces I've ever seen!"

Oh, dear, Ann thought, Sally has gone too far this time.

A slow grin worked its way across Seth's face, becoming an amused smile as it advanced. "So I've been told," he said. Lifting the infant from his shoulder, he added, "Here is your namesake. Guess we get to share her, seeing as we're the godparents."

Sally took the baby, admiring her tiny, perfect features and curly black hair. Soon Seth and Sally were completely engrossed in discussing baby Sally's progress, unaware that Ann existed.

Late that night the two friends, dressed in pajamas and robes, sat cross-legged on their respective serofoam mattresses. The babies slept peacefully in their cradles. The wood fire radiated comforting heat and the kerosene lamp gave off a soft yellow glow that highlighted the mellow logs and polished wood floor. Bolted for the night, the massive oak doors with their antique hardware seemed to insure protection while the multicolored preserve shelves with their canned green beans, yellow corn, beige apple sauce and dark blackberry jelly, added to the homey feeling.

"Not bad, rather cozy in here," Sally said, as she brushed her now loose, long brown hair. "You've done okay. In fact, I'm proud of you."

"Thanks, that is quite a compliment from you," Ann answered.

"Well, I wouldn't want to make it a habit, living this way. I mean hauling wood does ruin your nails and all those ashes must get into your pores, but still you look quite healthy, even without make-up. Must be the fresh country air."

"And you look simply stunning. Down to a slim sized eight, I bet. By the way, do you have a purse for every outfit?" Ann asked, recalling the red and white ensemble Sally was wearing when she first arrived.

Sally laughed, "A few do double duty. I'm rather a success."

"In line for sales manager?"

"No question I'll make that someday. I've already helped in increasing sales by ten percent. I seem to have a flair for arranging displays as well as motivating people. Great fun really. I'm enjoying it tremendously as well as spending all kinds of luxury money. Any time you change your mind."

A pang of jealousy touched Ann, for Sally was so successful and here she was on the brink of failure. It wouldn't be long before she would have to accept Sally's offer of a job.

"What about men?" Ann asked, another void in her life, along with money.

"Millions, I'm tripping over good looking young men on their way up. But none of them seems to be the right one. I don't know," Sally said reflectively. "That's why Mom has adopted your twins. She's given up on me."

Mrs. Canfield had made two adorable christening dresses, trimmed with fine lace. These she carefully guarded, until they would be proudly displayed on Sunday morning. Not wishing to share a cottage without electricity, Agnes Canfield was staying with Aunt Eva and Uncle Albert for the weekend.

"You'll marry someday," Ann said, convinced of her prophesy.

"I suppose so," Sally answered thoughtfully. "Right now I'm more interested in getting into new markets, experimenting with displays and sales promotions. And a lot of the men I meet are the same way, concentrating on their work."

"Jimmy Burns isn't like that, he adores you," Ann reminded her friend.

"Poor Jimmy. What he needs is a nice sweet girl. I'm not that nice; I enjoy maneuvering people too much. What I need is a forty years younger Seth Ruffles," Sally said, giving Ann a big smile.

"Oh, no," Ann laughed. "If you find one stay away from me. One seventy year old Seth Ruffles is enough for me. He has already won the heart of my baby; she only breaks into her dimple smile when he's around."

"And you?" Sally questioned, referring to the topic of men.

"Complete void," Ann answered, "In fact I've been so busy, I haven't given the subject very much thought."

"What about Roger Anderson?" Sally asked, well

aware of the two obviously expensive cradles.

"Oh, those. He's probably nostalgic about his one big accomplishment, this cabin."

"I thought he wrote for television, some popular day time program?" Sally questioned.

"He does and I imagine the results are very lucrative, if not high quality art."

Sally doubled over in laughter, waking the babies, who then had to be rocked back to sleep. "Boy are we getting fussy since we hit the road to independence," Sally whispered, once she had stopped laughing and the babies were settled down. "Or do we protest too much?"

"I don't know, I've never met him," Ann had to admit. "Anyway, dear friend, what I want to do right now is care for my two bundles of joy that we just rocked back to sleep. I want to be here with them when they learn all those smart things like feeding themselves and tying their own shoes. Some of the rest of life is just going to have to wait."

They spent a gorgeous fall Saturday fishing while the infants were cared for by their eager senior relatives. The two good sized fish they caught were inexpertly cleaned and fried for dinner over a hot wood burning stove. Their fresh flavor forcing Sally to admit parts of Ann's life style weren't too bad if taken in small doses.

On Sunday the big event went off smoothly. Eva and Sally looked adorable in their christening dresses and didn't object to Reverend Woodbind showing them off to the congregation. Baby Jimmy Westland was equally magnificent in Jim Senior's carefully preserved christening outfit. And when he gave the assembled worshippers a broad smile, over his proud father's shoulder, chuckles of delight could be heard throughout the sanctuary.

A potluck was planned for after the service, both to celebrate the christenings and to bid the snow birds a safe journey South. The food was plentiful and delicious and the talk especially lively; babies were admired, snow birds questioned about their winter plans and out of town guests introduced. Phyllis Westland and Sally Canfield took to each other immediately, their joking conversation, the combined care of one Ann Randall.

Agnes Canfield and Sally left shortly after the pot luck, with many hugs and promises to visit again.

Closing the door, Ann put the babies down for their nap, then allowed herself to feel the loneliness caused by the departure of her best friend. What fun we always have and what good discussion, she thought, as she wandered about the cabin unable to settle to any task. Walking by her desk she listlessly picked up her check book. A piece of paper fell to the floor. Retrieving it, Ann read:

> Onward with the noble experiment of one woman trying to raise a family in an outmoded, primitive manner.
>> I'm nosy,
>> Love you, Sally

A hundred dollar bill, having fallen from the note, lay on the polished wooden floor. Ann burst into tears. She cried for a long time, letting some of the worry and concern leave with her tears. Bless you, Sally, she said silently.

Now, buoyed by the thought that she could stay in Pinewood for a little longer, thanks to Sally's help, Ann set forth the next day to drop the babies at Aunt Eva's house while she purchased milk, eggs and butter for herself and the Gilberts. The girls weighed more than ever now, her arms ached before she was half way down the dirt road.

"There has got to be a solution to this before you weigh more than I do," she told them, envisioning a stroller for two or a red wagon with built up sides.

"Here, Uncle Albert," Ann said, putting baby Eva in his arms. "Baby Sally got so much attention over the weekend, I think Eva will develop a complex if you don't even out the loving."

Sitting in his wheelchair, Uncle Albert moved his arms to cradle the baby. Stroking her cheek gently with his permanently closed fist, he watched tenderly as a smile crossed baby Eva's face. "We'll sure remedy that won't we?" he cooed.

"Why don't you switch cradles?" Aunt Eva asked, between bursts of machine sewing quilt patches.

"Seth can tell the difference. Sally always gives him her dimple smile."

"Sally Canfield certainly looked marvelous," Aunt Eva said. Stopping her sewing, she turned to face her niece. "I hope you don't have any regrets," she added, with concern showing on her face.

"I miss Sally terribly, but I like living in the country. Besides how would you two get along without me?" Ann asked, to lighten the moment.

"We love having you here, that's for sure," Aunt Eva admitted.

Returning to the subject of everyday things, she said, "Would you see if Holly Fines has some cheddar cheese, medium. Albert has been wanting some Welsh Rabbit."

"Will do. By the way, Abner Gunther is going to hunt

on my land and in return, give me some deer meat. Would you like some?"

"We'd love it," Uncle Albert interjected, interrupting his baby talk with little Eva.

"Bring over the meat. We'll can it here," Aunt Eva said, not wanting to leave an inexperienced canner with such a valuable item.

"I was hoping you'd say that," Ann replied in agreement, as she started to leave for the grocery store.

Laughter was coming from the tiny village shopping center as Ann opened the door.

"We're missing a whole case of two inch nails," Holly said, trying to explain their hilarity, when she saw who had come in the door. "It is so crowded in here, Donald and I don't even know where everything is."

"I thought you put them on top of the refrigerator," came Donalds muffled male voice from behind stacks of produce.

"If I did they are not here now," Holly replied, undaunted by what must be a regular occurrence. Now concerned about her customer, Holly turned to Ann and said, "I hope you can find what you want."

"I should have no trouble. My whole list can be found in the refrigerator," Ann assured her. "Eggs, margarine, milk and cheese."

"Thank goodness," Holly responded. "I would hate to start looking for anything else. The nails are the second item we've lost today. Honestly, maybe what we need is a vacation."

"Found them," came Donald's triumphant voice.

"Where?" Holly questioned.

"Under the cereal shelf."

"I don't remember putting them there."

"Unfortunately, neither do I," Donald replied. "Your vacation idea is beginning to loom as a definite necessity.

Ann collected her groceries and carried them to the check out counter. By this time Donald was also there with his rescued nails, putting them on the hardware shelf behind the cash register.

"Ann, would you consider subbing for us once in a while?" he asked casually. "Holly is right, we do need a vacation. A couple of days off each month might do wonders for our organizational ability or lack thereof."

"You could bring the girls with you," Holly quickly interjected. "It isn't very busy here once the tourist season is over. You'd have plenty of time to care for your children and tend the shop.

"Why, why how marvelous!" Ann replied, her spirits rising.

"We would pay you, of course," Donald added.

"I'd be glad to help and I could certainly use the money. But what about your famous rolls?" Ann asked.

"I can make extra and put them in the freezer. I do that quite often. All you'd have to do is pop them in the microwave for a few seconds."

Ann walked out of the store thinking, a few more days, a few more days! Though the suspicion that the Fines were thinking of her needs as much as their own, didn't stop Ann from her momentary euphoria. Now the possibility of staying in Pinewood through the hardest part of winter was becoming a reality. Even if her typing service just brought in a little business, wasn't completely successful but produced some income, surely she could squeeze out a few more months.

Chapter 11

November came in overcast, damp and chilly. Except for the evergreens, the outside world was brown, with the brownness of frozen death. The nights started at five o'clock, sending the women to close drapes and turn on lights well before they put dinner on the table. There was idle talk of having a combined village Thanksgiving dinner at the church, for most of the men would be deer hunting and only dropping in to warm up and eat. But it was early days yet, decisions could be made later. Visits were quiet, people sipped coffee at friends homes, imparted news, discussed recipes, all in a state of waiting. The outside world seemed to be in this same state. The gardens were bare, the few remaining birds, chickadees, nuthatches and bluejays flew back and forth to feeders in a dull routine. Underfoot, soggy leaves had lost their crunch and wild flights and were now decomposing. No one talked about waiting, they just felt it, as country people do who live closely with nature. They watched the sky, smelled the air and pulled caps down over their ears or turned up jacket collars.

When it came, it came late. The wind intensified, making its presence known by sound in the dark night. Ann went outside to gather logs for the evening fire and felt its force on her solid oak door. Instinctively she went out again for three more arm loads, piling them up on the brick floor beside the bathroom door. Turning down the flue, for the wind had inflamed even indoor fires, Ann prepared for bed. As she crawled under her warm comforter and reached for her Bible, she was well aware of the fury outside the solid log walls.

Dawn was hardly noticeable, a dark gray light, blocked by millions of snow flakes that swirled against her south window. Out the east window, in the semidarkness, Ann could see spruce branches laden with snow. All day long it snowed, causing each home in the tiny village to comfort itself with electric or kerosene light, saying in effect, "This is what you've been waiting for."

The wind and snow died down the following day. The sun shown bright and clear on a transformed world.

Eager to see this new earth cover, Ann dressed the babies in warm clothing and tried to go outside. It was impossible, the snow was hip deep at her front door. Taking off their buntings, Ann left the girls inside, while she went out the back door and tramped through the snow to the old barn. Securing the snow shovel from its hook on the wall, Ann became aware of the extra lumber from the remodeling of her house, piled in one corner. Two, one-by-fours, four feet long, rested against the barn wall.

If I could make those into runners, I could have a sled, she thought suddenly. There is enough other wood to fashion a top with sides high enough to hold the babies' car seats secure.

Carrying the shovel, the two boards, and an old hand saw, Ann went back to the cabin. She shoveled the front walkway, then bundled Eva in warm clothing and took her outside for fresh air. All around them the trees were laden with white snow sparkling in the sunlight. Not a track was to be seen except for the ones Ann made. The old brown dying earth was transformed into a magic fairy land. Changing babies, Ann carried Sally into the woods close to the snow covered branches whose woven white patterns were an intricate display of loveliness.

In the afternoon, while the babies napped, Ann started shoveling the driveway, from the road inward. For thirty dollars, the county would plow your driveway all winter, but that was one luxury Ann had voted against; better she shovel than spend thirty dollars. The road had yet to be plowed, it was one of the last on the county schedule, for except for her, Seth and the cottages on the lake, there were no other homes on the road. The snow was light and fluffy, easily shoveled. Resting now and then, Ann, still enchanted with the view, discovered new vistas for admiration; white drifts against the wood pile, the crystal shine of tightly grown oaks on the forest edge and the snow cap on her bird feeder roof.

A four wheel drive pickup barreled down the still

unplowed road, its driver honking and waving as joyously as a kid on a fast sled.

Abner and May hiked over with Ann's first deer meat, meeting her just as she was ready to quit shoveling for the day. Over the usual steaming cup of coffee Ann heard the detailed news of the storm. The highway through town had been blocked most of the night and early morning, a wind battered tree had succumbed to the heavy snow and had fallen on the Smith's garage and the electricity had been out for four hours, causing many home owners to light their old wood stoves or fireplaces. This storm news was imparted with special delight as if the Gunthers had personally contributed to the village excitement.

The snow had brought new life to the village. Now talks of a joint Thanksgiving were positive. The men would all be hunting, Mrs. Jones and several other retirees would be alone and the village cooks would enjoy company in the kitchen. Therefore definite plans had been formed, naturally under Alice Ruffles' directions. Each person was to contribute a dollar toward the cost of the turkeys and each family was to bring a side dish or dessert. Children under ten would not be charged, leaving all the village youngsters, except the Gunther's teenagers, eating free. Duly contributing her dollar, Ann bid the Gunthers goodby.

Settling down with her wood and a pencil, Ann sketched curved lines on the two-by-fours in what she thought would be the proper curvature for sled runners. Then taking the old hand saw, Ann braced the wood on the edge of the brick floor and carefully sawed along the pencil lines. An hour later she had two roughly curved boards, the vital part of a homemade sled. Stopping for dinner and baby care, she then spent the evening trying to sand down the runners into a smooth unobstructed surface. By ten o'clock she gave up, there were still bumps and rough spots on the bottom of the boards and her house was covered with sawdust. Abandoning the runners, Ann set about building the sled top and attached sides. Hours later, she finally finished and was proud of the results. For the top only required sawing straight lines and nailing, tasks just within her ability and tool supply. Leaving the mess she went to bed. It must be two o'clock in the morning, Ann thought, too exhausted to even look at the time.

In the morning the sunlight revealed a home in chaos. Papers and wood were all over the floor, thick sawdust was on every conceivable area. What with the babies to care for, last night's neglected washing, washed and hung up to dry on lines over the bathtub and a house to clean, Ann didn't finish until well into the afternoon. There had been no time to make any further progress with the runners, they still stood propped against the preserve shelf, each bump and groove presenting an endless challenge.

Seth came to the door just as she was about to tackle the task of sanding down the boards. Without a word he went back to his truck, returning with a tool box of equipment, including a plane and a drill. By the time the babies were waking from their nap, Seth had the runners planed down and sanded, smooth as glass, the top secured to the runners and two holes drilled so that clothesline rope could be secured to the sled. Finally he took melted wax and liberally coated the bottom of the sled.

Together they bundled up the babies, secured them in their car seats inside the sled box and set off for a trial run. The road had been plowed, leaving a smooth hard layer of snow. The waxed runners glided over its surface with ease. Ann couldn't have been prouder if she had invented the wheel.

Even Seth grudgingly admitted he was impressed. "You'll make a woodsman yet," he said. Which she recalled was the closest he had ever come to a direct compliment.

They hiked the two miles to the lake, for Seth wanted to test the ice for fishing. The soft beauty of the winter scenery, her new found freedom and the babies delight with their ride, gave Ann an inner feeling of happy contentment.

No longer would she have to depend on others for transportation around the village or worry about the cost of gas if she took the car. And her days of carrying two growing children the mile to the Gilberts was thankfully over.

"Seth, you are a dear to help me so much. My back thanks you for smoothing the runners. I don't think I could have made one more trip to Aunt Eva's carrying these two."

"Used to make our own sleds, all the time, in the old days," he said, shrugging off the praise. Stepping on the frozen edge of the lake, he added quickly, "Think she'll hold. Should be able to do some fishing tomorrow."

Ann smiled inwardly. *He's so much more comfortable when we're arguing. He is positively embarrassed when I tell him how nice he is. What a dear sweet man.*

The lake in its smooth white blanket seemed twice as large as when dotted with fishing boats. Other than themselves there wasn't a soul around. The few cottages were boarded up for the winter, silent waiting buildings now exposed, as were the bare trees around them. There was no wind. The bright sun shining on clear new snow presented a picture of renewing peace. They walked slowly back to the cabin, not saying a word, just enjoying the silent companionship and the beauty all around.

With the first deep snow the village closed in, becoming almost an isolated island where only the school bus on its round trips to Hendersonville, the young people who worked in the larger town and the cars going in for supplies, provided personal contact with the outside world.

Each car going to Hendersonville went with lists of villagers' needs. On her monthly trip, Ann now found herself so overwhelmed with requests that she had to enlist the help of Beth Jacobson. The Jacobsons were without a car of their own, Winthrop's eyes being too poor to allow him to drive and Beth never having learned. So the arrangement was satisfactory for both women, now that Beth's passion for flower raising was restricted to indoor plants.

On Friday afternoons, while the infants slept peacefully on Aunt Eva's bed, Ann and Uncle Albert battled wits over the chess board. Ann struggled with the intricate moves of chess, but was so determined to give Uncle Albert a good game she even secured a library book on the subject. For Uncle Albert, with the ability to direct his moves verbally, - "queen to pawn four," - was able to participate in an activity well within his control. Though she seldom won, Ann enjoyed the mental stimulation and Albert's delight in winning.

When hunting week came it was a strange mixture of constant gun shots, unfamiliar trucks and vans driving the streets and blaze orange figures tramping the woods. Unless they too were hunting, the women and children remained near the safety of their homes. So it was with a mixture of excitement and relief to be out of the house, that Ann, on Thanksgiving morning, drove to the church, her car laden with babies and their needs and her contribution to the dinner. For safety's sake this was one time she would take the car on an extra trip, leaving the babies sled in the old barn. Seth, who had already gotten his deer, a ten pointer, would pick up Aunt Eva and Uncle Albert. The process of helping Uncle Albert in and out of the truck would be strenuous, but safer than walking the village streets. The men still hunting had been instructed to be at the church at two o'clock, or else! This directive had been given by Alice Ruffles the Sunday before and was not likely to be ignored, considering the reward for those who complied.

The village invasion extended to Thanksgiving dinner, for Phyllis Westland's mother, father and brother would be joining the community gathering, as they always hunted on Jim Westland's land. And a group of men from Madison, related to the extensive Ruffles clan, would also be sharing the Thanksgiving dinner.

Ann walked in the side door of the church and was met with white clothed tables in every available space. Over at one table Alice Ruffles and Will Sweeney were setting out silverware, while Beth Jacobson was arranging flowers at another and Aunt Eva was setting up the buffet table.

The delicious aroma of cooking turkey drifted in from the kitchen, along with the chatter of Marie Burton, May Gunther and Phyllis Westland, discussing how best to make the gravy.

"Hello Ann," Alice Ruffles said in cheerful greeting. "Let me give you a hand."

Instructing Will Sweeney to keep working, Alice left her table and helped Ann with setting up the play pen, removing jackets and carrying in two apple pies from Ann's car.

"I've got Will setting tables, as you can see. That should keep him occupied until some of the hunters arrive. Once they start telling their stories, he'll be in such awe, he'll forget to misbehave," Alice informed Ann, while they were outdoors removing the last necessities from the car.

"Good thinking," Ann agreed. "What do you want me to do?"

"Why don't you help in the kitchen? It is about time the potatoes were started," Alice replied, checking a list she kept in her apron pocket.

Gretta Sweeney had been in the kitchen, rather in the way of the cooks, but once she discovered the twins, she willingly became a model of good behavior. Eagerly she offered Ann the assistance of a four year old, not always a competent, but always a keen level of involvement.

Assured that Aunt Eva would supervise the young assistant, Ann accepted Gretta's help and took herself off to a potato peeling assignment. Gradually the buffet table filled with homemade apple, blueberry and pumpkin pies, molds of colorful jello, deep red cranberry sauce, hot rolls, direct from the oven, fluffy mashed potatoes and turkey gravy, yams in brown sugar sauce, corn, string beans and squash casseroles and finally two golden brown steaming turkeys, carried in by the men; they were so big.

The arrival of the hunters brought an even more

joyful atmosphere to the gathering. Several men had been successful, adding two more bucks to the food supply and numerous stories for the nonhunters and children to admire. The animated talk was now of points, rifles and sightings, only stopping long enough for Reverend Woodbind to give the Thanksgiving grace.

After the meal, Phyllis Westland's father led the group in hymn singing. When all were ready to go home, (some for a late afternoon nap,) the cooks, flushed with many compliments, agreed their idea had been splendid and they would surely make this an annual event.

By the second week of December, Ann was down to a bank balance of two hundred seventy-nine dollars and two cents, plus two dollars and fifty cents in cash. The cash was a payment for typing Jim Westland's letter to the University of Wisconsin's agriculture department and sixty dollars of the seventy-nine was for working at the Fines' general store for two days. There had been no response to her five dollar ad in the Hendersonville paper.

Carefully planning for Christmas, Ann weighed the cost of each idea and finally settled on homemade fudge for the Randalls in California and Christmas bread and fudge for Sally and her mother. These she would make with the supplies she had on hand and mail within the week. However she still had to purchase additional chocolate chips, carnation milk and butter for more fudge as well as candied fruit, cherries and nuts for additional Christmas bread, gifts she would also give her aunt, uncle and Seth. Ann had already knitted a dark blue scarf for Uncle Albert and was working on a pink and white knit hat for Aunt Eva, which she planned to finish in time for the holiday.

Her Christmas cards she would make from red construction paper, gluing on a spray of spruce needles for decoration. Inside, Ann would include a typed note to bring everyone up to date on the babies' progress. She planned to mail four cards: to the Randalls in California, to Sally and her mother and to Mrs. Smith and Mr. Appleby, but still this added another dollar to her expenses. The Pinewood and Hendersonville cards she would deliver by hand.

The village was in a frenzy of activity, each family preparing for its own Christmas as well as decorating the church in preparation for the Christmas Eve candlelight service. Everywhere, gaily colored lights were being strung, trees were being cut and carried home from the woods and extra car trips were being made to Hendersonville, for absolutely essential but somehow forgotten items. Fortunately for the travelers, the frequent snows were light, only falling an inch or so at a time.

Ann and the girls would be spending Christmas day with the Gilberts. They would be sharing one of the venison roasts, Ann's Christmas bread, mashed potatoes and gravy, several vegetables and salads and Aunt Eva's carrot pudding. One of the Gunther teenagers had kindly provided a tree for the Gilberts, a small one he had found in the woods when hunting for his family's tree. Ann could hardly wait to show baby Eva and baby Sally the gaily decorated tree, help the twins open their presents and record in her heart their very first Christmas.

There wouldn't be a tree in the log cabin. The only ornament Ann had, a chain made from left over construction paper, had been used to outline the preserve shelves. The Christmas cards she received she framed in spruce branches and hung on the louvered doors. Her three inch red candle she set on the dining table surrounded by spruce branches, pine cones and small red apples from the root cellar. Two additional candles were placed on the desk and the corner of the counter top, nestled in smaller branches, pine cones and tiny red bows made from scrap material. On her front door she hung a pine cone wreath with a large patchwork bow. Even without a tree her home looked festive; softly highlighted by the three red candles, decorated with nature's bounty and a few homemade additions, the spirit of Christmas prevailed over Ann's tiny home.

Christmas Eve afternoon was a traditional visiting time for the villagers. All preparations having been made, those families able to get out easily, dropped in on the elderly, handicapped or those with small children. This took the place of caroling, for by the last of December the nights were bitterly cold and everyone wanted to race for their home fires as soon as the church service was over.

On Christmas Eve day, Ann determinedly put aside her money worries, started the coffee brewing and arranged cups and cookies for her expected company.

The Gunthers and the Jacobsons arrived first, bringing with them a box of assorted homemade cookies and Christmas gifts for the twins. Over steaming cups of coffee, while the snow from their boots made little puddles on the floor, they wished Ann a Merry Christmas. Excitedly they described how beautiful the church looked with the addition of twelve poinsettia plants from the Andersons and a garland for the choir loft, which had just arrived from the McLaughlins. Gaily they told of their own home decorations and adventures in purchasing or making Christmas gifts.

Before they departed, Alice and Seth arrived. The merriment of this large group woke the babies, who, passed from loving arms to loving arms, smiled and laughed, joining the good cheer that permeated the room.

Still in high spirits, the country folk gathered again that evening at the church. Soft white candles illuminated the alter, ropes of greens hung before the choir loft where the red robed singers began the service with, "Oh Holy Night." Reverend Woodbind read the Christmas story interspersed with traditional Christmas hymns, sung lustily by the whole congregation. The service closed with the beautiful hymn, "Silent Night." Sending Ann home on her first Christmas Eve in Pinewood, joyful in heart for all God's gifts and especially for her children, home and this loving community.

Chapter 12

A blizzard hit the week after the holidays, stranding motorists, piling drifts four feet high against the south west side of buildings and permanently damaging weakened tree branches. Following the storm the temperature plunged downward reaching forty below at night and barely warming to a bitter twenty below during the day. Road crews were slowed by vehicles that refused to start and temperatures that made working outdoors dangerous.

Ann missed a doctor's appointment for her road was blocked and her driveway, laboriously shoveled out from the last storm was now a smooth white blanket, two feet deep. Having decided she would not take the girls out when the thermometer showed ten below or lower, Ann had found herself stranded at home, surrounded by a sparkling white world that gripped your breath the minute you dared step into the falsely beckoning sunshine. Her fingers and toes tingled from brief trips to the wood pile. It had taken minutes to disperse the freezing air that rushed in whenever the door was opened. Her hardwood floor felt cold to the touch, making it necessary to put a blanket under the play pen.

During the second week of arctic weather, Ann had found herself becoming restless; she missed the quilting sessions, the chess games with Uncle Albert, the visits from the villagers and especially church. No one seemed to venture out, only one four wheel drive truck passed in a two day period.

It became hard to be neat or keep the cabin clean. At the end of a day her scissors and sewing basket were left on the table, dishes were piled in the sink and the floor was marked with foot prints going back and forth from the door to the stove.

Ashamed that her house cleaning was so influenced by whether or not she expected company, Ann had risen that morning determined to have a spotlessly clean house. She washed the dishes, sink and bathroom, put away all working materials and was on her hands and knees scrubbing the wood floor with flax soap when the knock came at the front door.

She didn't believe her ears at first for the temperature was still well below zero. The knock came again. Brushing off her soiled jeans and pushing back her uncombed hair, Ann, scrub brush in hand, went to answer the door. It was a good thing she didn't have time to glance in the bathroom mirror for a dirt smudge ran from the corner of her eye, across her cheek to the tip of her ear. A small gray cobweb rested on her long curving eyelashes.

The man standing at the door was about six feet tall, in his early thirties, with the beginning of a black beard below a straight red tipped nose. His eyes were green, large and serious with a touch of reserve that was somehow appealing. He was dressed in a navy blue parka with a hood that covered his hair and came down to the edge of thick black eyebrows. In his gloved hand he held a brown paper wrapped package.

"Are you the person who advertised in the Hendersonville paper that you do typing?" he asked, beginning to look as if he was sorry he came.

"Oh, yes," Ann said, putting on what she thought was her most welcoming smile, hoping to reassure this stranger, for she must be presenting a very disheveled appearance. "Please come in. I've been cleaning. I'm afraid I'm rather a sight."

The man entered, without disagreeing with her statement.

At least the house is neat and clean, Ann thought defensively.

No sooner had he removed his parka revealing broad shoulders and narrow hips on a muscular frame, when baby Sally, tired of napping, demanded attention in the form of a loud cry. Not to be ignored, Eva joined her twin.

The young man stood and stared while Ann washed her hands, picked up both babies and tried to soothe them. Their combined vocalization continued, making conversation impossible. Unable to converse with her guest, Ann took time to change each infant and hopefully settle them in the play pen. Used to a week and a half of excessive attention, the babies weren't about to be satisfied with toys. In desperation, Ann handed baby Eva to the visitor.

"Here, please hold her for a few minutes while I put the coffee on. I'm afraid I've spoiled them the last few weeks. We've been pretty much confined to our own company because of the weather," she said apologetically.

Hesitantly he put his manuscript on the table, took Eva in his outstretched hands, held her there for a moment then with the most charming smile Ann ever recalled seeing, brought Eva slowly to his shoulder. The baby, secure in strong hands with an opportunity to look over a supportive shoulder, quickly ceased crying.

With Sally in one arm, Ann put on the coffee, obtained cups, sugar and cream and coming to the table, sat down opposite her guest.

"Not quite a business atmosphere," she said, "but I'm really quite good at typing, including spelling and punctuation, if necessary."

"That's nice to hear, spelling being my weak point," he replied seriously. Glancing around her home his eyes stopped at the two beautiful cradles, traveled across the preserve shelf, scrutinized the well maintained stove and came to rest on Ann. "You have a cozy place here."

"Thank you," she answered with a cool tone of voice, not pleased with his inordinate interest in her home. "I charge two dollars and fifty cents a page. Is this the material you'd like to have typed?"

"Yes. I've written a book, some three hundred pages," he answered, his green eyes twinkling with repressed humor. Which quickly began to annoy her for she couldn't see any humor in the situation.

"I could have your manuscript finished by the end of March. That is if you care to employ me," she said, anxious to know his decision. While at the same time wanting him to know that this was strictly a business discussion, regardless of her appearance.

"That would be fine. I would like to employ you," he said forcing face muscles to show a serious expression.

By now the babies were satisfied with being held and were quite happy to gain the freedom of the play pen.

Once coffee was poured, Ann took the brown paper parcel and opened it to the first page.

Foundations
by
L.R. Anderson

"I know Anderson is a very common name, but are you by any chance related to Alma Anderson here in Pinewood?"

"I believe so." He smiled. That smile that transformed his face into an expression of pure delight, sending her heart racing, in spite of her determination to be professionally formal.

When he didn't volunteer any more information, Ann returned to business. They discussed margin requirements, double spacing, location of page numbers and the fact that his last name must appear on the top of each page. Satisfied that she knew the necessary format, Ann turned to page one to be sure she could read his writing. A check for two hundred dollars, made out to her, was between the title page and the first page of chapter one.

"An advance for supplies," he offered.

"Thank you, that will help," Ann said, in what she hoped was a cool business manner. But inwardly she jumped for joy. Money, money, money, such a lovely commodity. Silently, while pretending to read, she multiplied two dollars and fifty cents by three hundred. Coming up with the grand total of seven hundred and fifty dollars. With clients like this her money problems would be over. Suddenly her world took on a rosy glow. The Good Lord was watching over them!

The first page of his book was written poorly with many a spelling mistake. A number of words were crossed out and pen printed letters were jammed between rows.

"Where can I reach you, if I have any questions?" Ann asked.

"I move about a bit. Why don't I stop by, say in two weeks. We can discuss any problems then." Rising, Mr. Anderson thanked her for the coffee and bundled up for his entrance into sub zero weather.

Ann watched him from the front window gracefully walk down her shoveled path, turn and stare at her home with a broad satisfied smile. Then leave, walking toward town.

Why is he so interested in this house, she wondered, a little apprehensively? Telling herself the book was legitimate, he appeared to be a clean cut, honest person and the check was written on a Hendersonville bank, convinced her not to worry.

Chapter 13

In early afternoon Ann heard the unmistakable sound of Seth's truck. Though the day was warming, now a mere minus ten, she was still surprised that he would venture out. She waited at the door ready to open it the minute he arrived.

"Why, you brave old soul. I'm glad to see you," she said, quickly shutting the door once Seth was inside.

"Would have been over sooner, but she wouldn't turn over," Seth replied, obviously referring to his truck. Giving Ann one of his rare smiles, he added, "Can't stay long, she might balk again. Then you'd have me here till the deep freeze passes."

"If you do have to stay, you get the wood hauling

duty," she threatened. How about coffee while you're waiting for Sally to wake up? That being the real reason you braved the arctic weather."

"Sounds pleasing," Seth answered, seating himself at the table.

Ann softly hummed a tune while securing cups, coffee and a plate of cookies.

"You seem mighty cheerful for someone who's been house bound for the past few weeks. Most of the village has a touch of cabin fever by now," Seth commented. A questioning frown crossed his face adding to the multiple wrinkles on his forehead.

"The most wonderful thing happened!" Ann explained, sitting across from Seth now that their refreshments were on the table. "A young man named L.R. Anderson brought a manuscript for me to type. A book with three hundred pages. Which means, seven hundred and fifty dollars! Which means I will make it to the middle of February! From then on I will have three hundred and fifty dollars a month from my bond interest. And if my typing service brings in some business, I can work at the store a few days a month and I can raise my own food, which I intend to do, I'll be a completely independent, self supporting, head of this household."

Seth laughed, "Well I do declare, you sure are a determined critter."

"And I intend to stay that way!" Ann announced. "That is," she hesitated. "That is if you'll show me the best places to fish."

"Well, now, I'm an independent critter too," he teased. "I'll go along with that idea for a nice fish dinner with mashed potatoes and gravy."

"You're on!" Ann willingly agreed.

Baby Sally opened her eyes and on hearing their

voices, immediately demanded attention. After a diaper change, Ann put Sally into her godfather's eager arms. There was several minutes of baby talk then Seth said casually, "Mighty nice of Roger to give you his book to type."

Ann had been tending to baby Eva's needs. Startled, she turned to face her old friend. "Roger! Roger Anderson! Alma's son?"

"Why sure. He's home. Came in last week out of the blue, so to speak. No one knew he was coming."

"But this says, 'Foundations,' by L.R. Anderson," Ann read the title page resting on her desk.

"He was baptized, Lawrence Roger Anderson," Seth said calmly. "I know, I was there."

"Why didn't he tell me? I even asked if he was related to Alma and he just said he believed they were related or words to that affect, as if there was some distant relationship. When I asked where I could reach him, he said he moves about and he would contact me in two weeks.

"Probably gets tired of women making a big fuss over him, cause he works with all those T.V. people," Seth answered casually, more interested in the baby in his arms than Ann's question.

"What a conceited ass!" Ann stormed.

Seth, now completely involved in lifting Sally up and down and watching her face light up in delight, ignored Ann's last remark.

For a half hour she stomped around the kitchen, preparing a fish chowder and muttering to herself. Then realizing her problem with Roger had nothing to do with Seth and that she was being a terrible hostess, she put aside her hostility and invited Seth to stay for dinner.

"Fish chowder, home made wheat bread and baked apple sound okay to you?" she asked.

"Sounds especially fine to me after what I've been eating the past few weeks. Worst of these cold spells is nobody asks you over for a meal. They think you don't want to venture out after dark. They give you a ring on the phone, tell you the village news, complain about the weather and forget your stomach."

"Oh, what village news?" Ann asked. Suddenly she realized how glad she was that Seth was staying and how lonely she had been the past week. When she went out to restock the wood pile, the temperature had again dropped below twenty below. Regardless of the cold, Seth stayed for dinner and helped settle the babies for the night, giving them both much needed companionship. When he went to leave the old truck gave a few sputters before grinding to a surprising start.

His departure left Ann free to begin work on the manuscript. She picked it up reluctantly, almost wishing she could afford to throw it in Roger's face. No wonder he was so interested in her home, he built it. No wonder he smiled when he looked at the cradles, they were his gift.

Who did he think he was that he couldn't be honest and open with her? Some king from Hollywood, way above these mere mortals that he condescended to help, now and then?

Still seething, Ann turned to the first page of his book, expecting to read about some glamorous sex symbol. Instead the words were about a small boy, a six year old, toe-headed, barefoot child going on his first fishing trip. Within minutes Ann had forgotten her anger. She was walking down that country lane with a man and his son. A lane that seemed exactly like the country paths of Pinewood.

Chapter 14

"Ug! Is that what you have to do?" Ann asked squeamishly.

"Oh, yes," Phyllis said smiling. "Here sit down and I'll show you how it's done."

Watching Phyllis clean out the chicken cavity, Ann questioned, "All of that has to come out and be sorted?"

"This is only a middle step. First the feathers have to come off. I dip the bird in hot water and hang it over there for that process. When I'm sure all the feathers are removed, I go to this step. The liver, heart and gizzard are useable. This one, this one and this one," Phyllis said, holding up each organ in turn and rinsing it in a pail of fresh water. "I like to package and freeze them separately from the chicken, but you'll probably cook them all at once, until you get electricity and a freezer."

Spring had come in surprising ways. Suddenly boots had broken through the hard crusted winter snow, little green shoots of grass had appeared in sun drenched, protected areas and streams of water had trickled down from roofs that had long been snow white. The spirits of the villagers had soared. Gardeners had inspected their white covered domain and had envisioned row upon row of healthy food producing plants. Fishermen had checked the lakes, found narrow bands of water between the shore and the massive ice and had imagined themselves hauling in bass from wave tossed water. The infirmed had looked out windows and dreamed of sitting outdoors, their aches and pains soothed by the sun's warm rays. Everywhere silent prayers had been given to the Lord for guiding them through another rigorous winter.

Anticipating the passing of snow, Ann had bought a second hand red wagon from the Gunthers and had extended the sides upward using leftover lumber. Drilling holes in her new means of transportation, she was able to secure the babies' car seats by passing the straps through the holes and buckling them on the outside.

Assured of a means of transportation around the village during the summer months, Ann had next tackled the project of preparing one end of the small barn for a chicken house. This had required building nesting boxes and roosting areas, as well as boarding up the end of the barn to make a closed in section. Fortunately there was a small side door at the end of the barn which she could use for an entrance to the chicken coop. The hen house completed, Ann had next cut a small door in the side of the barn, just large enough for a chicken to enter. Around this entrance she had erected a fence to give the birds an outside area, hopefully free from predators.

Now satisfied that her chicken house was adequate, Ann, one early morning in May, had punched air holes in a large cardboard box, bundled the girls in the car and driven to Phyllis Westland's farm, some five miles from Pinewood.

The Westland Farm was a beautiful dairy farm with a modern milking barn, numerous silos, a well kept farm house and extensive fields. Ann had found Phyllis in one of the many outbuildings and thus had found herself watching with disgust as the chicken was pulled apart.

Phyllis went over to the hanging rack and secured another plucked chicken. "Here you do this bird. Nothing like hands on experience, to make sure you remember the proper procedure."

"You mean nothing like hands on experience to help your friends with their more unpleasant chores."

"Naturally," Phyllis laughed. "I started this project because I knew you would be here today to pick up your beginning flock."

"Much more of this and I'll never eat chicken again. In fact I think I'll stick to eggs, cholesterol or no cholesterol," Ann said, bravely cutting open the bird and extending her hand inside, while unable to keep a disgusted expression from dominating her face.

Amused by Ann's discomfort, Phyllis kidded, "Come on city girl, this is the way we all get our meat."

"Okay, okay, I love country living, or most of it," Ann replied, unable to change her expression. With determination, if not desire, she carefully followed instructions until with a sigh of relief she could say, "There, I think your bird is done. Handing the cleaned chicken to Phyllis, she asked, "How many more do you have to do?"

"Just three and we can have a cup of coffee and some sweet rolls I made this morning."

"Now that's the part of country living I really like!" Ann replied, her expression improving from one of distaste to one of joy.

After the chickens were finally packaged and put in Phyllis' freezer, they spent a delightful hour sipping coffee, admiring their children and sharing village news. Then another hilarious half hour rounding up twelve half grown chickens, before Ann bid her friend goodby and started home with her first farm animals.

Ann had seen Roger twice during the long end of winter, other than casual greetings on Sunday morning. He had stopped at the cabin after the agreed two weeks, during a period when the babies were teething. As baby Eva and Sally were irritable and napping fitfully, they had had little time to talk, other than discuss business. Ann was able to present him with a hundred neatly typewritten pages. Receiving in return another welcome check. Too proud to ask why he hadn't told her his true identity during their first meeting, Ann kept her comments to technical questions about the manuscript, deliberately avoiding any personal questions that might be construed as, "fussing over him."

Roger remained serious during their brief discussion. Only when he was leaving did he venture from the topic of his book. "It's mighty pleasant in here, even with the babies fretful."

"Thank you," she had replied formally, while rubbing baby Eva's gums so that her fussing wouldn't drown out their conversation. Relaxing her cool manner slightly, Ann added. "I started with excellent construction."

Roger hadn't smiled or said, thank you, he just looked around her home with a thoughtful expression. "If the book sells, I might retire," he remarked softly, almost as if he were speaking to himself."

The second time she saw him was at the end of March. She had finished typing his novel and had placed the manuscript in a larger manilla envelope. The village news had been that Roger would return sometime in late March or early April to check his mother's house, for Alma was due to return from Florida by the end of April.

Ann had been in the front yard putting out bread crumbs for the birds when a large maroon car with gold lettering and the unmistakable grill work of a Cadillac drove onto her sandy driveway.

Roger had climbed out of the drivers side wearing a dark brown tweed jacket, a tan shirt open at the neck and dark brown slacks.

Her heart raced at the sight of his strong, handsome features and graceful movements until she noticed the woman sitting in the front passenger seat. Her immediate thought was that this must be the woman Phyllis described at the auction, for her hair was too light to be natural and her facial makeup was evident even from where Ann stood, some thirty feet away. Another couple was in the back seat, but Ann couldn't see them clearly.

Leaving the driver's door open Roger came swiftly to where Ann was standing.

"I hope you have the typing finished. I'm in quite a hurry," he stated, without bothering to say, "Hello."

Ann just looked at him. Again her heart began to race, but this time it wasn't from an overpowering attraction.

Speaking as slowly as possible she said sweetly, "You know, I believe I have finished your manuscript. I think I told you at the time you first employed me that I would have the work finished by March and I have done exactly that." Producing a broad false smile, she waited for his next comment.

"Would you please get it," he said, while extracting a check from his billfold.

"Certainly."

Before turning away Ann glanced toward the car and saw an expression of obvious boredom on the face of the overly glamorous passenger even though two strikingly handsome Purple Finches had arrived to sample the bread crumbs.

Strolling leisurely toward the house, Ann took as much time as possible to secure the manuscript.

By the time she started to return, Roger's impatience had reached new heights. He quickly came to meet her and reached out for the manilla envelope.

"Look, I'm sorry about rushing you like this, but we've just come from the Minneapolis airport and are on our way to a meeting in Chicago. I talked them into driving so I could stop and see if everything is okay at my mom's house before she heads back from Florida. They've gone out of their way to accommodate me and I don't want them to be late for that meeting."

"Why, of course. I understand. No problem at all," Ann said, smiling her false smile.

For a moment Roger looked confused, then

abruptly turned and moved swiftly to the car. Within seconds the Cadillac was out of sight, leaving a cloud of dust on the dirt road.

"How can he write such a beautiful story about the northwoods and be attracted to a woman like that?" Ann asked herself. She was feeling quite low now that they had left and she had no outlet for her irritation.

By the third week of May, Ann had planted her potatoes, onion sets and peas and readied the rest of the garden for the later vegetables that would be planted after all danger of frost was past. The twelve hens she had bought from Phyllis Westland were doing nicely, providing her with three or four small eggs each day. Best of all the twins were rosy cheeked and healthy seeming to blossom in the warm spring sun. As she pulled the red wagon over the dirt road to Aunt Eva's, Ann thought again of how grateful she was to be raising her children where there was freedom for young bodies to run and play, to breathe fresh country air and be amazed by the beauty of God's world.

Aunt Eva and Uncle Albert had offered to care for the girls while Ann spent the day fishing. They were in the side yard preparing for their day's companions when Ann arrived.

"How are my girls?" Aunt Eva asked happily, as she lifted baby Eva out of the red wagon.

She was greeted with outstretched arms and a few audible sounds, one she was completely convinced was, "Auntie."

Following hugs from Uncle Albert, Aunt Eva put Sally and Eva on an old, clean blanket stretched out on the lawn and practically covered with enticing toys.

After unpacking diapers, bibs and all the other baby

paraphernalia required and promising Uncle Albert her biggest large mouth bass, Ann left the contented foursome. On her way back past the cabin she picked up two fishing rods and quickly hiked the two miles to the lake and the shoreline where Seth had said she should fish for bass.

The point of land she selected was free of trees. Covered by rocks, sand and small vegetation, it made a perfect place to sit in the warm spring sun and cast out into deep water. Putting her jar of milk in the edge of the lake where the cold water would preserve its freshness and her egg sandwich in the shade, Ann then rolled up her jeans to just below the knees. Kicking off her sneakers she felt the pleasure of warm sand oozing between her toes. Baiting two lines, Ann propped one securely between two rocks and started casting with the other. Her hopes were high for a successful day, for both households were looking forward to the delicious taste of freshly caught fish.

Ann had just pulled in her first large mouth bass when she heard a twig snap. Looking up she saw Roger Anderson, fishing rod in hand, working his way onto the point.

"Hi," he said casually. "Guess we had the same idea."

He was dressed in jeans and an old flannel plaid shirt. Ann couldn't help noticing his impressively broad shoulders. Unwelcome feelings of masculine attraction she had tried to avoid for some time now, raced through her mind. "Curtly she responded, "There is room for two."

Roger's green eyes sparkled, his now clean shaven face broke into a smile. "Thanks," he answered cheerfully, mocking her obvious hostility.

Ann turned back to her fishing, wanting to blot out Roger's appealing eyes and delightful smile. Thoughts of Tom flooded her mind. Thoughts she had carefully suppressed since his sudden death last summer. It had been easy up until now to not think of Tom, for the struggle to survive had consumed her waking thoughts. But now with Divine help and dear friends she had made it, their future looked secure. True, it would require hard work on her part and careful management until the twins were in school and she could take a full time job. Still Ann was very proud of herself; she was free and independent and able to give her babies the start in life she felt was important.

I will not allow an attractive man to disturb my hard won goal, Ann told herself, absolutely denying the feelings Roger aroused. So forcefully was her mind demanding control that her muscles tightened, sending her cast plopping into the water just a few feet from shore. Yards of fishing line bunched around the reel, snarled in a hopeless mess.

"Oh, damn," she muttered.

"Here, let me help," Roger offered, seeing white nylon protruding from her reel in all directions.

"I'm perfectly capable of correcting my own errors," Ann said through clenched teeth.

This time Roger didn't smile. He observed her silently for a moment and then went back to fishing. It took Ann twenty minutes to straighten out her line. From then on they fished without speaking. If there was now a cool atmosphere between the only two people on the point, at least the fishing was good. By noon they had both caught their limit.

Pleased with her success, Ann secured her lunch. Selecting a flat, smooth rock she sat down, stretching out her bare legs to catch the warm rays of the sun and began to eat her egg sandwich.

"Do you mind if I sit here?" Roger asked sarcastically, indicating another smooth rock beside Ann.

"Go right ahead."

Seated, Roger opened a thermos of coffee. Pouring a steaming cup full he sipped the hot brew. "So, it's a lovely day, the sun is shining, the birds are singing, the trees are budding and we've caught some beautiful fish. So why the hostility? I'm beginning to think I have leprosy or something."

Oh, good heavens, Ann thought, have I come across as being that unfriendly? It really isn't Roger's fault that he reminds me of Tom and a marriage gone sour.

Lamely she said, "I just value my freedom."

"You mean the blackberry jelly and the cradles?" Roger asked.

"Well, yes," Ann answered, recalling how annoyed she had been when he hinted for blackberry jelly.

Roger heaved a sigh of relief. "The cradles weren't meant as a rich man's gift to the poor village back home. They were really a present to my house. And the jelly, I guess I was a little homesick at the time.

"Your house! I believe I payed you sufficient money to have it qualify as my house."

"Darn, there I go putting my foot in my mouth again," Roger said laughing. "Please let me try to explain before you run out on me again like you did last Sunday after church. With Abner Gunther and Seth's help, I felled every log in that place. I sweated buckets notching every joint. I mixed every drop of clay and placed each brick on that floor. All the frames and windows were put in place by these hands. There isn't a knot hole I don't know about nor a slightly warped board I couldn't locate with my eyes closed. I guess what I'm trying to say is that your house will always be part of me."

His words penetrated her defenses. "I know," she said truthfully. "I love it too."

"Then you understand why I couldn't completely let go? Why I was pleased that you couldn't afford to modernize, turn it into just another house? You see, you have kept my little boy dream alive. Every time I walk by the cabin or go inside, my ten year old dream world comes back to life."

Ann stared out across the lake. "I understand now," she answered softly.

"Good, then let's be friends. I promise not to give the house any more gifts."

"Fair enough," Ann laughed.

A fish jumped in the middle of the lake sending expanding circles across the smooth surface. There was a feeling of peace and new birth in the air. Stretching out her legs to bask in the sun's rays, Ann felt a lessening of tension. Perhaps she and Roger could be just friends after all and she could go on blocking out the past forever.

"I would like to say that you have nice legs," Roger commented, "But I won't. It might make me sound chauvinistic. But just for curiosity's sake, as an abstract question only; why do some women look so appealing in patched jeans and others look like nothing at all in five hundred dollar gowns?"

"The answer is; in the eye of the beholder," Ann replied.

Quickly she rose to collect her fishing rods, not wanting the conversation to become personal, even in a roundabout way. For she was aware there was teasing laughter in Roger's voice when he talked about an abstract question.

"I had better get back. Aunt Eva and Uncle Albert have probably had their daily share of tears and diaper changes by now."

"And I had better get one of these fish to Mrs. Jones before she has a chance to make me an orange butterfly or a purple cow." Roger sighed as he headed toward their fish. "By the way, I would offer to carry your fish if you wouldn't be offended by my male "gallantry.""

"Fine, I'll carry the rods. They're much lighter," Ann agreed calmly, ignoring his teasing attempts to get her to react.

Watching his graceful athletic movements as he walked to the edge of the lake to secure their fish, she thought, you might ask the same supposedly abstract question about men. Why do some men look so masculine and attractive in patched jeans and old faded shirts? Forget those impressions she told herself. Let him think you're a liberated woman who's not interested in a man in her life. That should keep him at a distance. Play up that angle and you'll be safe. Safe from falling in love again. If you don't fall in love, you can't get into fights about what is important in a marriage; you can't get hurt. Simple as that!

They walked back leisurely on the old sand road. "Will you be returning to Hollywood soon?" Ann asked.

"I have a leave of absence for two months," Roger answered. "After that I don't know. But what about you, why did you move up here?"

"Aunt Eva and Uncle Albert are my only relatives on

my side of the family. After my husband died, I wanted the babies to be near family," she answered casually. Ann was fully aware that they were both being evasive, neither giving the complete reason for their actions.

She was speculating on the real reason he was home when they came abreast of the log cabin. Parked in the driveway was a bright red convertible, obviously not out of the show room for more than a few days.

"Sally!" Ann shouted with joy.

For who else but Sally would own such a sporty car? Dropping the rods, Ann ran for the house. Sally had just put her overnight case by the couch when she heard her named called. The friends flew into each other arms.

"Oh, Sally, what a great surprise!" Ann said happily. "But why didn't you let me know you were coming?"

"You're missing a few modern conveniences, remember, no phone. Besides I thought it would be fun to surprise you. I finished my business in the Twin Cities and have a couple of days before I'm due back in Hampton. By the way, old chum, what is that smell?"

Ann drew back hurriedly. "Sorry, it's fish. We've been fishing," she answered, hoping she hadn't left any permanent odor on Sally's smartly tailored, cream colored suit.

"And this is the proof," Sally commented, noticing Roger quietly waiting in the doorway with two strings of fish. "Mighty nice looking fish, almost worth the smell."

"Sally Canfield, this is Roger Anderson," Ann introduced.

"You're the Roger Anderson who writes for, "Loves of My Life!" Sally exclaimed. "I've seen your picture in our brochure. I work for Allen Cosmetics and we provide the make-up for your television program. Gosh, what great fun meeting you!"

"Same here," Roger replied, breaking into his charming smile. "Your cosmetics are first rate. I would shake your hand but I'm rather loaded down," he added, indicating the collection of fish.

"I'll take mine out back," Ann offered. "They'll have to be cleaned right away."

"Why don't we clean mine too and have a big fish fry in honor of Sally's visit," Roger suggested. "We could pick up the kids and your uncle and aunt and have a party."

"Do include Seth, he's one of my favorite people," Sally added, eager to begin planning.

"First however, I must do my duty by Mrs. Jones," Roger remarked, carefully selecting a fish for that purpose.

"Why don't we take my car, drop off Mrs. Jones' fish and pick up the rest of our party? I can't wait to see my gorgeous godchild," Sally offered.

"You haven't met Mrs. Jones on her own turf, have you?" Roger asked, a chuckling sound in his voice. "Come on, let's go. Maybe I can get her to give you the pink cow instead of giving it to me."

"She sounds suspiciously like an over exuberant crafter," Sally said as she and Roger headed laughingly for the red convertible.

Leaving Ann with a mess of uncleaned fish.

Chapter 15

At least cleaning the fish was easier than it had ever been. Ann was hardly aware of cutting off the heads, so busy was she thinking of Roger and Sally. They were both full blast, out in the world people, she thought. They would go well together. Sally would be much better for Roger than that bored sex symbol sitting in the front seat of a rented Cadillac, Ann decided. Not for a moment would she allow herself to be the slightest bit jealous.

The party arrived all at once. A carefree laughing group of people swarmed into the house, including the Westlands, whom Sally had called and encouraged to join the fun.

"Seth and I will cook. Fresh fish is man's work," Roger announced. "Where is the frying pan, Ann?"

"I'll set the table," Sally offered. "Ann, where are the place mats, silverware and napkins?"

"Ann, do you want these potatoes sliced or cubed, jackets on or off?" Jim Westland asked.

The next hour was a bustle of activity. Everyone moving in all directions around the tiny cabin.

"Well, Seth, if you would stay over by the stove where you belong," Came kiddingly from Sally, when the two collided.

"I would stay by the cooking if you weren't constantly butting in, checking on my work," Seth retorted.

Finally the fish was served and eaten amid grudging compliments to the fishermen, cooks and servers. The babies were composed for sleeping and a group of contented adults began settling themselves for a time of quiet conversation. The one kerosene lantern on the dining table gave off a soft glow, the wood fire sent a cozy warmth around the room. Seth and Aunt Eva moved their chairs to face the quilt covered sofa. Ann was about to sit on the sofa when Roger sat at one end. Leaving the other half for Sally, Ann sat on the floor beside Phyllis and Jim with her back propped against the louvered closet doors.

The talk remained light and cheerful. Everyone was too content from the satisfying meal and pleasant company to think of any annoying topic. Gradually Ann became aware that Roger spoke very little. Instead he listened to what others were saying. Sally talked long and intimately about her job, Seth revealed some of his past, even touching on the painful loss of his wife and usually quiet Jim Westland regaled them with the antics of his barnyard animals. Roger's questions and comments were brief, but always kind and understanding as if his emotions were in accord with whomever was speaking. He radiated an atmosphere of loving acceptance that subconsciously drew everyone to him. In spite of the delightful evening, Ann was thankful when it was over. She was finding it extremely difficult to keep up her defenses against such a caring man.

After their company's departure, the two friends settled down for the night. The twins were sleeping soundly, exhausted from all the attention they had received. Sally sat Indian style on her bed brushing her long golden brown hair. In the soft glow of the lamp, Ann rested on her mattress, filing her nails.

"How could you be lucky enough to meet a man like Roger Anderson in this little town when all the men I encounter on my world travels seem to be pot-bellied and bald," Sally confided, giving her friend a - tell me all about it - smile.

"You don't mean that!" Ann said laughing. "You've already written me about at least three men who fit the description of perfect."

"Don't evade the issue. You kept Roger at arms distance all evening. In fact you practically threw him in my lap. Not that I wouldn't mind, but why the rejection?" Sally asked bluntly.

"I'm not ready, I guess," Ann said thoughtfully.

"Well, it can't be because of Tom. You hardly saw him once you got pregnant. Every time I stopped by he was out with the guys. You're not still in love with him, are you? You didn't act that way after his death. I mean you weren't completely devastated."

"After he died I knew I had to take charge," Ann began slowly, knowing Sally was forcing her to face her inner feelings. "Besides, at first it didn't seem real, his being gone. It was as if he were out somewhere, or at work. Later I was too involved with providing a home for the twins, to think about the past.

"It's time you did, you know. You're not blocking off Roger because you still care that much for Tom. I think you're rejecting Roger because something was wrong with your marriage," Sally said forcefully, wanting to jar her friend into facing her real feelings.

"I suppose you're right. We weren't getting along very well," Ann said, putting down the nail file and snuggling under the covers.

"I know you got pregnant sooner than you'd planned, but you and Tom would have worked that out. Once the babies came you would both have been so thrilled you would have forgotten they were a year or two early."

"Sally, the conflict wasn't over my being pregnant so much as the fact that I wanted to stay home with the children for their first few years."

"Tom wouldn't go along with that idea?" Sally asked in surprise.

"No. He thought I should go right back to work after the babies were born. I know it would have been hard to live on his salary, especially with house payments. But we could have managed for a few years; lived with second hand appliances or gone without a new car. I just wanted to stay home until the children were in school. Tom thought we had already sacrificed enough by saving for a house; he had no intentions of continuing to do without."

"Oh, Ann, I'm so sorry. I had no idea you two

disagreed that much. But Tom was saving for a house, at least up until the time he decided he needed a new Thunderbird."

"Sally, Tom was saving for a house until we started arguing, after that his extra money went into nights with his friends. Those last months, I was the only one saving for a house."

"You were building up to a divorce?"

"I don't believe in divorce, except in unusual situations. No, I would have gone back to work as soon as my maternity leave was over. But I don't know what our relationship would have been like after that. I think, something vitally important would have been missing. The bond of understanding that really binds two people together would have been destroyed and I'm not sure it could be rebuilt."

"Oh dear."

"What would you have done in my place? How would you have felt?"

With Sally settled under her covers, Ann reached out and extinguished the lamp, leaving them to continue their conversation in the now dark cabin.

"I really can't imagine what I would do. You see, I have Mother. She would love to help if there were grandchildren. I would feel completely at ease leaving my children with her."

"Yes, I can see where you would feel that way. Your mother is a sweetheart."

"You know, now that I think of it, Mother never worked outside our home. She was always there to see us off to school and greet us when we returned home. I had a wonderfully secure childhood," Sally said reflectively.

"My mom always said those were the best years of her life, the years when I was a baby. She told me she used to rock me to sleep in a big chair by the garden window. She could look out and see Dad working with the flowers and look down and see me sleeping and think that she couldn't possibly be any happier," Ann said softly.

"Ann, why didn't you tell me about Tom?"

"After he died, I wanted to forget everything, to block out all my fears. I was doing very well until Roger came along."

"But this time it could be different," Sally said encouragingly.

"I can't take it that lightly. I can't just turn around and give my love and trust."

Though Ann was revealing her soul, she began to feel better as if finally admitting her pain, made it easier to bear.

Chapter 16

By the first of June there was a complete change in the tiny village of Pinewood. The church quilting day was canceled for the summer. Leisurely visits over coffee and cookies ended, replaced by quick conversations while inspecting gardens or asking advice on how to eliminate some fungus or pesky garden bug. Too environmentally aware and too money conscious to use pesticides, most village gardeners used old home remedies passed on by word of mouth.

The population swelled to around two hundred, now that the summer lake cottages were occupied. Sophisticated women in shorts bought baskets of prepared foods from Holly Fines' crowded store, while their children played in the village square. Tanned young men, tired of water skiing, stopped for cases of coke, then raced off in fancy cars. The village handymen were busy every day, repairing winter damage on lake front property, mowing lawns and providing wood for cottage fireplaces.

Alice Ruffles, quick to see the advantages of adding tourist dollars to the church coffers, organized an ice cream social. Ignoring the protests of the overworked gardeners, she assigned jobs to the entire congregation. Even the minister's wife, Sara Woodbind, was pressed into service with the dubious honor of scooping chocolate ice cream. Ann and Phyllis Westland were assigned the craft table, a task Alice was sure they could handle and still care for their infants. This momentous event was to take place on Saturday night during fourth of July weekend. A date Alice calculated would see the greatest number of summer visitors. Ann was not eager to take part in this fund raiser, but like the rest of the congregation, knew there was no escape. Too busy with her first year of gardening, caring for baby chicks and the serious need to provide fish for both families, plus the constant care of her children made her hardly aware of the changed atmosphere. True she did awaken in the middle of the night when tooting cars raced down her usually quiet road. Moaned when there was a long line waiting to make purchases at Holly's little store and worried when motor boats disturbed duck families on her fishing lake. But these were only fleeting concerns; she was too involved to give much thought to the summer people.

Fortunately the tourists preferred casting from fishing boats, leaving the point to Roger and Ann. Without any set agreement they found themselves fishing together each Thursday morning: sometimes in lovely soft sunlight, occasionally in torrential rains or misty fog blanketed mornings. Sometimes they talked leisurely of village affairs, other times they fished in silence, and on rare occasions they got into heated political discussions. But, by silent mutual agreement they avoided any reference to personal matters. Each week Roger was casually friendly, never prying nor overly complimentary. Gradually Ann was able to relax and enjoy their mornings together, knowing the physical attraction between them would be ignored.

Roger's book had been sent off to a publishing company. While he waited for a reply, Roger played chess with Uncle Albert on Saturday evenings, helped Seth with his haying, mowed Mrs. Jones' lawn, adding to his felt collection, ran errands for his mother and generally integrating himself in the life of the village.

The evening of the ice cream social was calm, hot - well into the high eighties - , without a cloud in the sky. Just the weather Alice Ruffles had ordered. All afternoon the grumpy villagers had sweated over setting up tables, running errands, arranging plant displays, fresh flower arrangements with price tags attached, craft items - unfortunately including Mrs. Jones' contributions - and buckets of dry ice to keep the ice cream under control. Unconcerned with their obvious attitude, Alice, having a bigger picture in mind, directed the setting up with the determination and endless energy of a general. She put Roger, with his film of rehearsals of, "Loves of Our Lives," in Abner Gunther's garage, next door to the church. The craft table she ordered placed by the church door. The plant, flower and fresh vegetable tables she had scattered about the front lawn and the ice cream, cake and cookie tables under the one shade tree.

Uncle Albert and Abner Gunther were assigned the woodworking table at the beginning of the church front walk. Here Uncle Albert could answer any questions while Abner sold bird houses, wall shelves and small picture frames. Alma Anderson, Aunt Eva and May Gunther were in charge of the cakes and cookies, while Marie Burton was placed next to Sara Woodbind, assigned to scooping vanilla ice cream.

Not until the first young tourists arrived, fresh from their afternoon swim, did the spirits of the villagers improve. The eager delight of their young visitors suddenly made the afternoon drudgery all worthwhile. Raggedy Ann dolls went into eager arms, ice cream and cake disappeared into hungry young mouths and parents bought bird houses and plants, magnanimous with the pleasure they were providing their children.

Unusual designs in homemade quilts were carefully examined and admired. Purchase prices, well beyond the sewers imaginations, were accepted. City people, eager to have possessions that were not turned out uniformly in the millions, wrote checks for homemade quilts and carried their purchases away with a look that said, "I now have warmth for my spirits as well as my bed."

Slowly but steadily old cigar boxes filled with checks, bills and coins, adding much needed revenue to the village church.

Gretta Sweeney, tired of helping her grandmother at the ice cream table, came over to the craft table where there was the added attraction of three babies. Willingly she rescued thrown toys, played fun little games to make baby faces laugh and eagerly offered cookies to Sally, Eva and Jimmy.

"You're a wonderful helper, Gretta," Ann said to the four year old.

"Isn't she!" a lady, purchasing a corn cob doll, agreed. "Just like my granddaughter."

"I know", Gretta replied proudly.

As the soft glow of sunset eased the intensive heat, torches were lit and dark shadow areas heightened the festivities. The young parents with their wide eyed children were replaced by a free adult crowd. Men that Ann recognized as hot rodders and young women in shorts with beautifully tanned bodies, now drifted about, mingling with the senior citizens in from their evening's fishing.

Jim Westland came in after finishing the milking chores and with the help of his mother took the three babies to the Westland home for the evening, leaving Ann and Phyllis free to help until the end of the social.

Shortly after the babies left, four year old Gretta climbed onto Ann's lap and within minutes was sound asleep.

A steady stream of women and some men crowded into the garage. Ann could hear the questions asked of Roger whenever the film stopped.

"Is it true that her salary will be a million dollars next year?"

"Don't you just love working in Hollywood?"

"Is he really that good looking? I mean in real life?"

"It must be so much fun to work with all those glamorous people!"

When Alice Ruffles finally gave the signal to close down, the entire working congregation gladly complied. It was well after ten o'clock. All of the baked goods and all of the ice cream had been sold and most of the other tables had only a few items left. Even some of Mrs. Jones' concoctions had disappeared.

The remaining tourists were all crowded around Roger, who had closed down the film room and moved outdoors. Ann could see him patiently listening to a group of men and women still eager to bask in film land's reflection. Slowly two of the young women in shorts with beautifully tanned legs drifted closer to Roger's group. The conversation became more animated, laughter permeated the night air and a sense of renewed energy radiated from the group. A nearby torch lit up Roger's smiling face as he conversed with one of the young women.

Ann carefully eased the sleeping child onto her shoulder. "Phyllis, I'm going to take Gretta home and put her to bed. I'll be right back to help clean up."

"Okay," Phyllis replied, beginning to pack up their few remaining items.

Ann stopped by the ice cream table to tell Marie Burton that she was going to take Gretta home.

"Oh, thanks," Marie said, lethargically, showing the strain of the day. "Just give me a minute to finish wiping this table and I can go with you."

"I'll do the table," Sara Woodbind offered. "You go ahead with Ann. She can help you get Gretta tucked in bed and then you take a rest yourself. The Reverend will see that Will gets home."

The Burtons lived in one of the houses facing the town square. It only took a short time to carry Gretta home and help her grandmother put her to bed. But when Ann returned to the ice cream social, the avid group of television enthusiasts had completely disappeared, including Roger Anderson. A weary cleanup crew was all that remained. The women were packing boxes and folding up table cloths while the men took down tables and chairs and the few older children that remained, gathered papers from the church lawn.

"It is suddenly very quiet around here," Ann remarked as she carefully folded up the two remaining embroided pillow cases.

"A welcome relief. I'm about worn out," Phyllis replied. "Though it turned out to be a great success. We should have no trouble paying for that new church furnace."

A new furnace wasn't exactly what was on Ann's mind. "Did Roger finish packing his equipment?"

"A while ago. He has gone off with the Brady group. Those people who have that huge place on Perch Lake. I think they're from the Cities. They were certainly having a laughing good time when they left here."

Phyllis reached across the table to hand Ann the unsold pot holders. Even in the dim torch light she could see that she had said the wrong thing. "Well, not exactly a laughing good time, actually. Just friends getting together. Probably went back to the lake for a cup of coffee," Phyllis corrected, trying to soften her remarks.

Reverend Woodbind came up to their table. "Here, let me carry that box for you," he said. "I'll put it in the church. And thank you both for all your hard work. We have certainly added a sizeable amount of money to the church coffers today. There should be no trouble at all putting in that new stove."

Uncle Albert, Aunt Eva, Phyllis and Ann walked back down the dark street to the Gilberts, lighting their way by flashlight. All a bit weary, they walked in silence. Ann was glad it was dark and no one else had the energy to carry on a conversation, for she had something to say to herself and that was, that she had been very silly. Very silly to think for a moment, even in her subconscious, that

Roger could possibly be more than a friend. That Roger could be at all interested in her, other than as a companion, based on her house and the fact that she had settled in his home town.

The truth was that Roger was just being kind. As he had said, the cradles were nothing more than a gift to the house. And why not? Anyone would be proud of building such a sturdy structure.

The manuscript probably had more to do with Alma Anderson than Roger. She would be the person who knew Ann was advertising for typing work and would know about Ann's tight budget. Alma had, most likely, thought of her involvement as a help to Ann and a convenience for Roger.

Face it Ann, she told herself, the truth is you are the one who was falling in love. You're the one with stars in her eyes, imagining all kinds of romantic dreams, that will never be. Roger lives in a glamorous world of mansions and sports cars, far from the farming world of feeding chickens and hoeing string beans. His stop here with his mother is just a temporary rest.

Do grow up, she continued, determined to rid her thoughts of any fanciful ideas. Roger is a friend and that's all. Enjoy his company while he's visiting his home town and hope he writes more books so you can add to your income.

Chapter 17

Carrying her fishing equipment, Ann walked leisurely toward the point. The day promised to be hot, but as yet the early morning shadows kept the road comfortably cool. Her thoughts were pleasant. She looked forward to Roger's companionship, enough fish to do some canning and hopefully, time for a swim.

Roger was already fishing when she reached the point. Two large mouth bass circled in his creel.

"You're here early," she greeted him cheerfully.

"Have to be, this time of year. They won't bite when the sun is overhead."

"Mum," Ann responded, settling down to bait her hook and get her line in the water.

They fished silently for over an hour, concentrating on the task. By ten-thirty the sun was beating down on the point and on the still, crystal clear water. Even the bluegills gave up nibbling on their bait and headed for deeper water.

"Let's take a coffee break, then try further down where there is some shade," Roger suggested.

"Fine with me," Ann agreed, having caught several good sized sunfish. At least assuring tonight's dinner for both families.

"How did we make out on the ice cream social?" Roger asked as he handed Ann a mug of coffee.

"Very well! We can easily pay for the new stove and Reverend Woodbind thinks we'll have enough left over to refurbish the pews."

"Oh, good!"

"The quilt sale brought in the most money and your film was next. Most people do like to know about Hollywood," Ann added while slowly sipping her coffee.

"That's because I was there and could give them inside information they would never have heard otherwise. Adds a bit of spice," Roger replied with a touch of humor in his voice. Reaching over, he refilled Ann's coffee mug. "Were you and your husband movie fans?"

"Not really. Tom and I went occasionally, but mostly we went dancing and to parties before we started saving our extra money for a home of our own."

"It must have been hard to lose your husband and your home," Roger said sympathetically.

"We hadn't actually gotten that far, that is, far enough to purchase a house. But we were almost there; we'd started looking at houses. That's why the log cabin is so dear to me; it's my very first home. I like feeding the wood fire and knowing I'm keeping my family snug and warm. I like sewing and making the twins attractive outfits and I like rocking them to sleep in those beautiful cradles you gave us. I love everything about my home. Home is such a vitally important place."

"I agree with you there. Home is our anchor, our comfort and our refuge. When you're reaching out, trying to achieve something in the world, thoughts of home give you security and support." Roger opened his picnic basket and offered Ann a piece of his mother's homemade coffee cake.

Ann accepted the delicious looking coffee cake. "You know, I even think there would be less crime in our country if more women would stay home and make the home and the church the important part of their lives," Ann said, warming to her favorite cause and forgetting all about asking Roger if he could explain Tom's point of view.

"Well, you certainly live your beliefs. Here you are staying home with your children and living a homestead life. So all is right with your Pinewood world," Roger remarked, beginning to feel that he might be in for a long lecture on a subject he had never even considered. Quickly he suggested, "Come on, let's try fishing in the shade."

Without waiting for a response, Roger picked up his fishing rod and headed toward the water.

They worked their way along the rocky shore, where the trees grew out of the hillside, arching their tall bodies over the water. Even wading in the lake a few feet required side arm casting. An hour of careful effort only produced three keepable sunfish.

"What do you say to quitting and taking a dive in the

lake?" Roger asked, as he rescued his line from an overhead branch.

"Brilliant idea," Ann answered heartily, the day's heat already producing beads of perspiration on her arms and forehead.

Swimming leisurely, floating, diving to inspect an underwater world, they wallowed in the luxury of a cool refreshing lake. The experience of using their young muscles in new free ways brought emotions of pure healthy joy.

"Gosh, I feel great!" Ann said, as she waded to shore.

A splash of water hit her on the back. Turning she received another splash full in the face. Laughing, she struck back, spraying water over Roger's head, drenching his hair. Like the children in Roger's book they gave themselves completely over to the game. Worldly responsibility was gone, only the fun of scoring a direct hit mattered. Laughing, ducking, scooping water, they advanced closer and closer to each other.

Suddenly Ann's ankle twisted on a loose rock, sending her helplessly falling forward. Reacting instantly, Roger reached out, supporting her from going under water and helping her to regain her balance. For a moment their eyes met. The adoration in his was unmistakable. Wonder and excitement filled Ann's very being. At that moment, she would gladly, joyously have gone into his arms.

Roger's muscles tightened. Forcefully he drew his eyes away, focusing on the distant trees. Once her footing was again secure, he said huskily, "We had better go."

On the walk back, they both tried to recapture the light bantering friendship that had served them so well up until now. But throughout the casual conversation, Ann's inner thoughts churned with new wonder. In spite of all I've said about caring for my own children and in spite of all the exciting, glamorous women Roger is in contact with every day in Hollywood, he does care for me! There was no doubt in her mind, she had seen love shining from his eyes.

Chapter 18

The next day Roger was gone. Ann learned of his sudden departure when she went to play chess with Uncle Albert. She had dressed the girls carefully in newly made play suits, wanting them to look their best for Aunt Eva and Uncle Albert.

"You're both adorable," she told them, feeling quite happy and joyous herself.

The twins giggled in response. But quickly shifted to yelling, "Go, go," once Ann started buckling them in the red wagon. They had come to love these outings, beginning to be aware that the red wagon meant fun and extra attention from doting relatives and friends.

A short bumpy trip down the dirt road and the three

Randall girls were greeted by a delighted Aunt Eva.

"You two get prettier every day," Aunt Eva declared, giving each twin a hug. "New play suits! Isn't your mother good to you. They look so nice Ann, you did a splendid job."

"Thanks, my sewing is improving. I'll be able to make ball gowns by the time they're eighteen."

Showing off the twins newest accomplishment, Ann held baby Sally's hand while Sally walked with unsteady steps to Uncle Albert's wheelchair.

"Come on, come to Uncle," Albert encouraged the unsure child. "That's my girl," he said when they had reached the chair and Ann had lifted the baby into his arms.

The walking demonstration successfully given by both twins, Aunt Eva and Ann set up a play area in the Gilbert's shady back yard.

"I'm going to visit Alma Anderson today," Aunt Eva said, reaching for a basket of goodies she would take with her. "Alma will be a bit lonely now that Roger has gone back to Hollywood."

Taking an inordinate amount of time to settle the twins, Ann fought to control her emotions, to hide any reaction to the news. Waves of sorrow, loss and depression swept over her. Gritting her teeth she deliberately let her mind recall all the lonely evenings when Tom was not at home. Determinedly, painstakingly she rebuilt her solid wall of defense. The wall that had been crumbling slowly, brick by brick. By the time she bid Aunt Eva goodby and contemplated the chessmen, she was almost back in control of her own private world.

"You're not concentrating," Uncle Albert accused, after he had won the first game in three moves.

"Play again?" Ann tried to be cheerful.

"Upset over Roger's leaving?" he asked.

"No, of course not!" Realizing this sounded very false, Ann added, "I'll miss him on fishing days."

"He'll be back," Uncle Albert said confidently.

Who cares, she tried to tell herself. By the third game Ann's efforts at concentration were paying off. She didn't win, but at least Uncle Albert had stopped grumbling about her sloppy play.

They had just started their fourth game when one of the Gunther's old cars pulled into the driveway. Simultaneously, May and Abner alighted from the battered ten year old Oldsmobile. Together they advanced toward the chess table, announcing as they came, "The blueberries are ready!"

It sounded like a battle cry, as indeed it was! Without wasting any time on pleasantries the Gunthers launched into the village plan. Seth Ruffles would pick up Ann and the twins at seven-thirty in the morning. She was to bring everything needed for a day of gathering, including as many containers as she could find. Aunt Eva would ride with the Gunthers, while the Jacobsons and the Woodbinds would share another car. As the Westlands lived on the way, they would take their own vehicle and meet the party at the blueberry patch. That would leave Uncle Albert and Alma Anderson keeping each other company, with one of the Gunther teenagers across the street repairing a car, in case they needed assistance.

The party would not include Alice Ruffles, for she was on the County Board (as you would expect) and the County Board was meeting on Saturday, the very day of the blueberry picking expedition. The anguish of a born director over this conflict can only be imagined.

"Now bring lunch, snacks and lots to drink. The berries are in the burnt out area where there is little shade," Abner Gunther directed, filling in very nicely for Alice Ruffles.

Early the next morning, Ann piled her little family into Seth's truck. Soon leaving any habitation behind, Seth drove down one lane dirt roads that turned and twisted so often Ann was soon hopelessly lost. Part of the time they drove through dense forest, other times past opened pasture and still other times through scrub country where a few scraggly jack pines protruded above low undergrowth. The road dipped and climbed into valleys and over rolling hills sending the truck churning through pockets of sand in low areas. As the truck rose to the top of a new hill, Ann was suddenly faced with a sea of blackened tree stumps, eerie statues of decay. Reminders of the fierce fire that had once raged through acres of this forest land. Only new small vegetation gave any life to an otherwise desolate world that stretched to the horizon.

Off at a distance, in the middle of this desolation, she could see a tiny group of cars. When they arrived at this oasis of humanity, Ann found that the cars were parked so as to provide shade for the infants in the party. Leaving one adult to watch the children, the pickers fanned out quickly, buckets in hand.

What appeared at first to be a dead world, Ann soon discovered was teeming with life. No longer choked by trees, the berry bushes grew profusely in the open sandy soil. Lush blue fruit cling in bunches on short brown stems, appearing to offer themselves to a hungry world.

Off in the distance deer browsed contentedly on new green shoots, close by rabbits scurried before the human invasion while chipmunks voiced their annoyance and small green snakes slithered into the underbrush.

Ann quickly set to work picking the plentiful fruit. The

hot July sun beat down on her head, her knees became sensitive from kneeling in the rough sand and her back began to ache, but she ignored these distractions. Visions of preserved wild berries, blueberry pies, muffins and the dark fruit topping a bowl of cereal kept her muscles working.

Her second two quart pail was almost full when she heard Sara Woodbind yell, "I'm taking a coffee break."

Slowly the other pickers joined Sara in the shade of the cars, bringing with them their buckets of prized berries. Sprawling on old worn blankets, the group relaxed with mugs of coffee and fresh donuts. Not having Alice Ruffles to direct them, they leisurely ate and drank, while kidding each other about the amount of fruit gathered and complaining about the occasional bugs.

Ann glanced across the open fields. She was sticky from dried perspiration, her muscles ached and yet she felt content. Looking at her chipped mug, the old blanket she was resting on and her patched cut-off jeans, visions of her childhood returned.

The little yellow house on the corner, up the hill from the Methodist church. How filled with sunlight had been the rooms and her room especially with its two windows and pink clown wallpaper. Pink wall covering that had been put on when she was an infant and remained because she had asked to have it stay.

Her mother and dad who had been such loving, cheerful people whose lives were guided by their church, their home and Dad's job at a local grocery store. Nothing glamorous sounding from the outside, but inside there was warmth for body and soul. The look Mother and Dad gave each other when they greeted at the end of a working day, the smiles on Sunday morning when they met other church members and the happy songs sung by the living room piano.

So many little things that made your heart glad. The red mittens Mom knitted and surprised you with on the first cold day. Ann remembered them distinctly, bright red with cable all the way from the end of the cuff to the finger tips, exactly matching the red in her winter parka.

Dad's pride in his flowers. The pleasure he took in his little back yard garden and the fun he had presenting them with his cut selections for the day. Sometimes a large bouquet for Mom and a small one for her, that she could put on her desk by the back window that overlooked the garden.

Of course it hadn't been perfect and it had ended abruptly. Suddenly her parents were gone, the little yellow house burned to the ground and she had lost her foundation and her beliefs.

Sitting quietly, Ann thought of her childhood in one composite picture and knew that here in this Wisconsin village, she had found both the freedom and the security that was essential for her soul. The security she thought she had found when she married fun loving, joking Tom and his promise of their very own vine covered cottage. But this was not a promise, this was real. And because the environment was right she knew she would continue to grow here. Grow to care deeply about the people. See Aunt Eva as someone she sincerely loved and not just an aunt she could turn to because she was family. Admit in her heart that she respected and cared about old Seth. And feel for the first time in her adult life that she was truly a part of a lasting community, because it was a community based on faith in a loving God. If this did not include the love of a man, Roger's love, then she would still be grateful for what she had.

Chapter 19

At ten o'clock that night a siren sounded throughout the village of Pinewood. An eerie frightening sound that rose to a nerve shattering intensity, then receded, only to rise again. Please don't let it be Uncle Albert, Ann thought, knowing the ambulance had turned off the main highway and was making its way into the village. For minutes the noise came from a stationary place, then slowly diminished as the ambulance raced off, heading for the hospital in Hendersonville. There was no way Ann could find out what had happened. It was long after dark and the twins were sound asleep. Without a phone she could only wait until morning and hope that whoever was taken to the hospital could be helped by doctors.

Reasoning that if it were Uncle Albert or Aunt Eva, someone would surely come to tell her, Ann put aside her fears. Plunging her hands back into the sink full of water, she continued to clean berries. She had started canning blueberries that evening in order not to have the wood stove going in the heat of the day. It was a long slow process, made slightly easier because she could use the hot-water-bath method for fruit and therefore didn't need to use a pressure cooker. Still she had to work long into the night.

No cars came down her road, the village appeared to have settled back into its peaceful routine. Just the occasional song of a Whippoorwill disturbed the silence.

Eighteen pint jars of berries, displayed on her storage shelves was her reward at three in the morning. Added to the rhubarb sauce and peas she had canned earlier in the summer, the display was beginning to look substantial. Soon she would be able to add string beans to her years supply of food, a crop that always grew profusely and when preserved would most likely fill an entire shelf. Mentally Ann reviewed her expected supply as she wearily prepared for a few hours sleep. Canned vegetables would be peas, beans, corn and some beets and carrots. The fruit would be blueberries, apples, rhubarb, blackberries, raspberries and wild plums. Their protein would have to be eggs, chicken, fish and venison. The venison she would have to put up in quart jars, along with some fish, but now that she was raising chickens, this meat could be provided when needed. The root cellar would hold her potatoes, squash, some apples and fresh beets and carrots. This year would be a renewed challenge, for the girls were now eating regular food, forcing Ann to refigure the quantities she would need to last until next year's harvest.

Thankfully she was doing well with money: with the bond interest, several additional typing assignments from Hendersonville businesses and some work at the store, her expenses were well within her income. Once the girls reached school age there would be additional costs, but by then she would have her typing service well established, or if not, would be able to take at least a part time job. Pleased with her present success and future plans, Ann fell into a deep sleep.

The twins woke her in the morning. Shaking their crib rails, repeating, "Mommy, Mommy," they were bright eyed, ready for the day. Sleepily she looked at their happy faces, momentarily without appreciation. A weary glance at the clock indicated she had overslept by an hour. With effort, Ann hurried to dress, feed Sally and Eva, care for the chickens and generally get back on schedule.

The soft knock on the front screen door came as a surprise. The villagers were too busy this time of year to pay morning calls. Going to the door Ann saw Alice Ruffles and four year old Gretta Sweeney. Alice's expression was one of sadness, Gretta's mostly fear. The little girl's straight blond hair was combed, she had on clean shorts, shirt and sneakers but her frightened hazel eyes and her down turned mouth clearly indicated something was seriously wrong.

"Come in," Ann offered. Knowing that Alice would need the right moment to explain their visit, she kept the conversation casual. "Do you have time for coffee?" she asked leisurely.

Fortunately the twins were still in their high chairs, happily smearing jellied toast over their faces and trays. Silently, Alice watched Gretta become intrigued with the smiling, jelly faced babies.

"Perhaps we should," she answered, without taking her eyes from the young child.

Ann put the coffee pot on, thankful that there was enough morning fire left to heat the water.

"Gretta's grandmother went to the hospital, last night," Alice began, now that Gretta was busy handing the infants gooey pieces of toast.

"The ambulance last night?" Ann asked.

"Yes. The ambulance took grandmother Burton to the hospital. And now she is in heaven with God. I know she will miss her family, but she is very happy to be with God," Alice said slowly, watching Gretta carefully as she spoke.

The little girl had wandered over to the collection of toys Ann had readied for the outdoor play pen. Her back was toward the two women. It was impossible to tell her reaction to Alice's comments.

Sipping coffee, Alice continued cautiously, "Grandfather Burton has a weak heart and has to be very careful. Gretta knows he can't take care of children by himself because of his heart condition. So the boys are staying with the Jacobsons for a few days and we wondered if Gretta could stay with you for a little while?"

"Of course," Ann answered, endeavoring to make her voice cheerful, while inwardly trying to figure out how she could manage. Going over to the four year old, Ann put her hands lightly on the child's shoulders. "Would you like to stay with us, Gretta? You could help me with the babies."

The child shook her head, "Yes," without taking her eyes from the stuffed teddy bear she was holding.

Returning to her coffee, Ann whispered, "Any other relatives?"

"Attempting to find out," Alice mouthed silently.

After Alice left, Ann took the children outdoors. She settled the twins in the play pen under a shade tree and gave Gretta several small pails and an old spoon to use for digging in the sand. The child hadn't spoken, but seemed content to fill the pails with soft loose soil, giving Ann a chance to spend time in her garden.

That afternoon the Jacobsons dropped by with Gretta's brothers and took everyone to the beach at Fawn Lake. This was a small, but perfect beach for young children, for the sand eased out gradually into crystal clear water. Just about every village child had learned to swim at Fawn Lake and therefore it was considered the old village swimming hole, even though there were some thirty other lakes in the area.

Once the Sweeney children were playing in the water the adults could talk without fear of being overheard. As Beth and Winthrop Jacobson were in their late sixties, they wisely brought lawn chairs to make child supervision as comfortable as possible.

After the chairs were set up and the Sweeney children were involved in hunting for attractive rocks in the shallow water, Beth began. "We all expected Wilber to go, what with his weak heart, and here it was Marie. A few chest pains and she was gone. I still can't believe it! Why, she was dead when Winthrop and I got there, long before the ambulance came. Naturally they tried to revive her on the way to the hospital, but they couldn't. We knew it was too late the minute we saw her."

"How is Wilber?" Ann asked.

"Not doing very well at all. He is quite upset and

confused. May Gunther is over there with him right now. We really feel he shouldn't be left alone."

"Oh, dear. What will happen?" Ann asked.

"I think, myself, he will have to go into the Hendersonville nursing home. He just can't stay by himself in that house," Beth answered.

"I agree," Winthrop said. "He is in no shape to live alone."

Ann excused herself and took Eva and Sally into the water. The lake was too inviting to be ignored for long. They splashed and giggled and kicked their little feet with pure delight. After a time, when goose bumps appeared on their arms, Ann put them back on the spread out blanket by the Jacobsons.

Refreshed, she sat on the edge of the blanket and asked in a soft voice, "What about other relatives?"

"There is Wilber's brother, but he and his wife are almost as old as Wilber. I don't think they had any children. Did they?" Winthrop directed the last question to his wife.

"I don't think so. Marie has two sisters though and I'm sure they both have children."

"Perhaps one of Marie's nieces or nephews will be able to take the Sweeney children," Ann suggested, voicing all their thoughts.

"I certainly hope so," Winthrop replied. "We're too old to care for two active young boys. I'm worn out already just trying to keep them from turning our house upside-down.

"The Westlands are going to take the boys for the weekend if they don't find relatives by then," Beth said, trying to soothe her husband.

For a time the three adults watched silently as the children played in the familiar village swimming hole.

Being children they were unaware of the ramifications their grandmother's death would produce in their young lives. Perhaps it was just as well that they could enjoy this moment, for even if they were aware that their home might be permanently dissolved, they would have no voice regarding a substitute home.

The weekend came and went, the funeral took place, Wilber Burton moved to the nursing home and still there was no word about other relatives that might take the children. The Burton home stood idle, the grass grew high, the shades were drawn day and night and the house took on a deserted look.

The Westlands kept the two boys, visiting Ann as often as they could so that the Sweeney children could be together.

Ann became quite fond of little Gretta. She was a quiet child, solemn and serious, willing to play for long periods by herself. Only at night when Ann prepared a bed for her from one of the serofoam mattresses, did the child open up and talk.

"I like it here. Am I going to stay here or am I going home again?"

At first Ann had said, "I think you are going to go and live with some wonderful new relatives. Maybe your grandmother's niece or nephew. Perhaps in a house with dogs and cats and other children to play with."

But now that over a week had passed and there was still no word, Ann wasn't sure any longer that caring relatives could be found.

Gretta had also asked about her grandmother and they had talked of heaven and how marvelous it must be. Absorbing their talks without crying or showing any other emotion, Gretta seemed to be drawing into herself. Ann could only hope that in time and with a settled home, the child would be able to show her feelings.

During the second week, following Marie Burton's death, the authorities took over. Within hours, Gretta was taken from Ann's home and the Sweeney boys were taken from the Westlands. Ann had thought seriously of keeping Gretta until they were absolutely positive that there were no relatives that could take the children, so fond had she become of the serious little girl. But the social worker would not consider the possibility. The agency had found a foster home down state that would take all three children and this was deemed to be the best possible arrangement.

A brief hug goodby. A few silent tears when she said goodby to the twins and Gretta Sweeney was gone. Her tiny little hand held firmly by a stranger with momentous authority.

Chapter 20

"So they took the kids," Seth remarked, coming in with a cardboard box filled with assorted jars of honey.

"Yes. It nearly broke my heart to see Gretta go. She's such a sweet little girl," Ann answered sadly.

"A lot like her grandmother."

"Now that you say that, she does remind you of her grandmother," Ann said reflectively. Adding after a pause, "I was hoping the Sweeney children could stay in the village until relatives could be found. All this wrenching change can't be good for them."

"Think they would have found relatives by now, if there are any to be found," Seth said philosophically.

"I suppose you're right. I guess I just keep hoping

some wonderful couple, with a big house and dogs and cats will suddenly show up and be delighted to take the children."

Carefully taking out each jar of honey and putting it on the table, Seth remarked, "Good year, you won't need to buy much sugar."

"They're beautiful!" Ann exclaimed, admiring the rich golden color that shown from reused mayonnaise and jelly jars. Holding one up to the light, she asked, "Are you sure you can spare that many?"

"My bees are doing so good, I might even give old lady Jones a jar. Though fat chance of getting a supper out of her."

Ann laughed, knowing Seth's propensity to trade for a good home cooked meal.

"Take the girls and go fishing?" he asked, when the box was empty.

Surprised at his sudden suggestion, Ann questioned, "Do you have the time?"

"Roger got my garden in such good shape before he left," he answered evasively.

Aware that Seth had become as fond of Gretta as she had, Ann readily agreed. It would be good for both of them to take time off and adjust to their loss. They needed to relax with a fishing pole and let their spirits revive. Trying not to think of the traumatic experience Gretta must be going through at this very moment, Ann prepared the twins for the outing.

The weather had changed in the last few days, overcast with clouds and temperatures barely in the seventies, giving them a good chance of catching fish in the late afternoon. Putting an old blanket on the ground well up from the lake, Ann settled the babies, hoping they would stay within its perimeter. For a time baby Sally and Eva played happily within the confined space, but once they discovered the blanket had no restricting sides, they crawled off to taste the wonders of dirt, twigs and sand. Finding it impossible to fish and watch the children, Ann gave up and sat with them on the blanket. Seth caught several bass before joining Ann's family.

"Good to just sit and look at the water," he said reflectively. No sooner were the words out when both little explorers climbed up on his lap.

"If you can even see the lake with those two climbing all over you!" Ann responded.

"I can feel nature's peace, even if I can't always see," he said, tickling baby Sally so she would release her strangle hold on a lock of his hair.

"It is nice here, isn't it?" Ann said, watching a loon family swim into open water. "Roger and I always came here to fish. When it was too hot for the fish to bite, we swam off the point. The water is quite deep there and crystal clear, you can see minnows and bluegills swimming around the stems of water lilies when you dive under."

"He's a good man," Seth said, watching Ann out of the corner of his eye. "You couldn't do better."

"I don't need a husband, I can manage by myself," Ann retorted, quick to guard her newly erected defenses.

"Mostly, you can depend on God's people, though not always. A few of God's people make mistakes and a few are fair weather children, but overall God's people are faithful," Seth said mildly. He was seeing through all of Ann's protests, knowing she was really afraid of being hurt. "My Sara didn't believe. She thought you should take what you can get out of this world because this is all there is. She left me for a time and only came home when she was dying of cancer. I didn't care much about people after that, until you came along. Something about your spunk, the way you were determined to take care of your little family, kind of gave me a new feeling about women."

This sweet, ugly old man, Ann thought. And I never knew. I just assumed he had a loving, faithful wife who died before her time. No wonder he stopped going to church, no wonder he looked like he would like to bite your ear off. How awful to have a wife return only because she was dying and needed someone to nurse her.

Smiling his ugly smile, Seth continued, "Along the way, I also learned I needed God and I couldn't give up on life. And neither can you. So you give Roger some thought, young lady. No matter what blows come our way, God is here to hold our hand. All you have to do is ask for His help."

Ann reached over and gave him a kiss on the cheek. "I always take your advice. You're so wise."

Gales of raucous laughter burst forth from his reddening face. "That will be the day, that will be the day," he kept repeating.

By late summer, life had settled down to a familiar routine in the little town of Pinewood. Many of the summer people had left, their cottages boarded up for the winter. Harvesting and canning were going on full blast in every permanent household. Amid eighteen hour days of labor, Phyllis Westland and Ann were making plans for a first birthday party. A big gala event that would include the entire village population.

The evenings were always cool now, the days bright, hot and sunny or wild with violent thunderstorms. It was during one of the heavier storms that Ann discovered the old barn was leaking right over the chicken coop. On her morning rounds she had gone out to feed the chickens, to find the flock huddled in a corner while streams of water splashed down on the roosting bars and onto the straw floor. When the storm passed and the sun dried the soggy ground she put the twins in their play pen under a shady branch of the big oak tree and propped an old ladder against the barn wall.

Ann looked up to the roof line, telling herself that it wasn't terribly high, that there were a lot of other roofs that were a great deal higher. After all this wasn't an apartment building; it was just a one story farm outbuilding.

Tentatively she eased her way up the ladder, not at all comfortable with heights, but knowing the roof must be fixed or her precious flock would become ill. A fleeting thought of asking Seth to do the repairs crossed her mind as the old ladder moved under her weight. Dismissing this idea, she forced herself to continue climbing and to concentrate on what was wrong with the roof.

An inspection showed five shingles missing and three more in decay. All the damage appeared to be concentrated at the back of the barn, the rest of the roof looked in reasonably good condition. Ann climbed carefully down the ladder and went inside the building hoping to find something she could use as temporary repair material, until she could purchase new shingles in Hendersonville. There was no stored material that would be adequate for the purpose, but there were strips of tar paper nailed to the inside walls. Ann removed a section of the tar paper that she felt would be large enough and with hammer and nails in her pocket and the paper under her arm, she slowly climbed the ladder again.

At the top she stretched the tar paper over the area of missing shingles and reached in her jeans' pocket for the hammer. At that moment her weight shifted causing the ladder to slide sideways. Grasping for the roof edge, Ann tried desperately to steady the ladder top. Her attempt was unsuccessful. With increased speed the ladder slid sideways off the roof and crashed to the ground, sending Ann helplessly plunging to earth. Knocked unconscious when her head hit a rock, Ann lay helplessly in the boiling sun.

A sharp excruciating pain coming from her right leg brought her back to consciousness. Looking down she saw the tip of bone protruding through red flesh. Observing her leg with horror, she was only dimly aware of the sun beating down on her aching head.

We are here all alone, no telling when someone will stop by, Ann realized as panic mounted. I'm completely helpless, there is no one to care for the babies or to help me. Tears of pain and fright welled up and cascaded down her face. God in heaven, please help us, she prayed. Again she passed out, lying useless in the baking heat.

Slowly the cries of the twins came through her fogged brain. Rising painfully on her elbow Ann saw that the shade was no longer protecting them. The sun had moved to beat mercilessly on the plastic floor of the play pen. You must help them, her addled brain demanded. God give me the strength.

Slowly, inch by inch she crawled on her arms to the sun baked cage, dragging her swollen, broken leg. Several times her brain stopped working, collapsing her on the ground. Each time the cries of her children forced her to consciousness and a renewed effort. When she finally reached the babies, she used her last ounce of strength to push the play pen closer to the tree trunk into the blessed shade. My prayer for strength has been answered, she thought gratefully. Then she collapsed completely, only dimly aware that if help didn't come soon they would all die, she from loss of blood, the children from long exposure to the hot burning sun, for just one thin, overhead branch was protecting them.

Strong hands were holding her battered leg, placing a board under it and wrapping cloth tightly around and around. She could feel the powerful, competent hands but her eyes wouldn't open, they seemed weighed down by rocks.

"It will be all right, love," came from a deep masculine voice.

"Roger, Roger!" part of her brain screamed. What is he doing here? Am I dreaming? Did God send Roger to help us? With endless effort she forced her eyes to open. There he was, his black curly hair bent over her leg, powerful arm muscles working to wind white strips around her aching limb.

"Roger, you've come in answer to my prayer," Ann said with all the strength she could gather. The words came out as a whisper.

He heard the sound and looked up, his sparkling eyes intense with concern. "I have to take the twins to Aunt Eva and then I will be back for you," he said huskily. "Can you hold out a little longer?"

Too weak to speak, she barely nodded her head, tears of relief blurring her eyes. A gentle kiss touched her forehead.

"Come on girls, we are going for a ride," Roger announced, taking a twin in each arm. There was a slight whimpering sound from baby Eva. A reassuring, "You are my brave little girls." And then silence.

Ann came back to consciousness when Seth's truck bounded down the dirt road. She was lying on a mattress in the back of the pick-up, Roger by her side, holding her hand.

"We will be on pavement soon," he said when her face contorted with each painful jolt.

"I always seem to be going to the hospital in Seth's truck," Ann whispered, trying to smile.

"Seth will behave this time, he is accustomed to accidents. Only when babies are expected does he panic," Roger said, unable to suppress a grin. Recalling the tale his mother had told of the mad ride to Hendersonville when Ann was in labor.

"You came back to Pinewood. Why did you come back?" Ann heard herself asking.

"To marry you," Roger said matter-of-factly.

Chapter 21

The leg was set, a cast molded in place, then the blessed comfort of a clean white bed and pain killers lulled her into a deep sleep. Just before Ann gave into her need for rest she dimly heard the doctor say, "At least six weeks." Oh, no, was all she thought before the powerful drugs took over.

Ann woke to the cheerful voice of the nurse requesting she hold a cold thermometer in her mouth. Minutes of testing went by before the thermometer was removed and she could ask, "When can I leave?"

"The doctor will be in to see you this morning," came the evasive, standard reply.

Darn, I've got to get out of here, Ann decided once

the cheerful woman had brought her breakfast and left her in peace. *Why couldn't I have broken my leg after the harvest was over? How am I going to finish the canning and dig potatoes with this leg in a cast?*

Thought you could take care of yourself, didn't you? Ann started arguing with herself once she had consumed every scrap of food on the tray. *Free and independent, no need of help from anyone. Ha, look at you now!* Never mind, her other half countered, *you've gone through rough times before, you'll make it. With God's help, you'll make it.*

Don't panic, just plan. The first plan is to get out of here and stop that hospital meter running. This has probably already cost me more than my little savings account.

Thank heavens for Roger. The thought of what might have happened if he hadn't come that very day, sent chills throughout her body. *What had he said in the back of the truck? Surely it couldn't have been, "I came back to marry you." I must have been delirious to think that.*

Slowly Ann eased her plastered leg over the side of the bed. The leg throbbed as blood circulated to her foot. Gingerly she reached for the crutches beside the bed and eased herself to a standing position. For a moment that was all she could do. When her head cleared, her strength returned and she was able to take a few tentative steps. Thinking, crutches forward, hop, crutches forward, hop. *Amazing what a strain there was on her shoulders.*

Ann was working her way back to the bed when Doctor Durand entered the room. "Good for you. Up and at 'em," he remarked, watching her hobble back to the bed.

"When can I get out of here?" Ann began bluntly. Doctor Durand had delivered the twins, she didn't feel there was any need to be subtle with this forthright middle aged man.

"You're in a hurry? What is the matter, don't you like the food?"

"When the twins were born I had medical insurance. Now I don't."

"Can't afford it I suppose," Doctor Durand said matter-of-factly. He was showing no sympathy at all, which in a strange way was why she liked him. "You think medical insurance is expensive, you should try paying my malpractice insurance bill," he muttered while continuing his examination. Her heart was checked, the leg examined, questions asked, the chart read and finally he looked satisfied.

"Do you have anyone to help you at home? I don't mean for an hour, I mean all day." He stared at her, his brows wrinkled, his look demanding an honest answer.

"I'll find someone," she said confidently.

"Hum. How much money can you spare?"

"I have two hundred dollars saved and I should be able to manage an extra fifty each month."

"I would guess the hospital and lab costs would come to about a hundred and fifty dollars. You pay me twenty-five dollars and a bushel of apples and we'll call it even."

"Apples!"

"I hear you have good cooking apples and I love apple pie," Doctor Durand said defensively.

Ann laughed. The good old country bartering system extended as far as Hendersonville. "A deal," she said happily. "I'm going home and plant more apple trees."

"Not on that leg you're not. And you can check out

this afternoon on one condition, that there is someone at home to help you. I don't want you back here tomorrow, exhausted from trying to do a full days work, when you have just broken your leg. My wife would throw me out if more than a bushel of apples showed up at her door."

Once the doctor left, Ann quickly dialed Aunt Eva.

"Dear, how are you? We were all so worried."

"My leg is in a cast from my hip to my toe. It pains a little, but otherwise I'm okay. Do you think someone could pick me up this afternoon?"

"So soon, shouldn't you stay at least another day?" Aunt Eva asked in surprise.

"Doc Durand said I could go home if there would be someone there to help. Do you think Alma or May or even Alice could spare the time? You must be worn out with the girls and Uncle Albert."

"Don't you worry about us, we're doing fine. But I'll see what I can do." Aunt Eva's voice became vague, along with her answer.

"Is everything all right?" Ann asked, knowing Aunt Eva's tone of voice meant she was trying to hide something.

"What did you say, dear?" Aunt Eva questioned, as if she were stalling for time.

"Is everything all right?" Ann repeated. "The twins didn't have any burns, did they?" she asked in dread. Surely she hadn't been unconscious for long, had she? Or had the babies been exposed to the hot sun for hours while she lay helpless, not even hearing their cries. Ann remembered crawling to the play pen, forcing it back against the tree. But that was all she remembered until Roger came. Had she lain there for hours while the hot sun shifted, sending its deadly rays to burn young tender skin?

"Your children are fine," Aunt Eva said, now with a firm positive voice. "I have to go, dear. See you soon."

The phone went dead before Ann could reply. Why was Aunt Eva so evasive, Ann wondered? There was something wrong and if it wasn't baby Eva or Sally, what could it be? Aunt Eva was a kind, understanding person, but always direct unless she was trying to avoid imparting bad news. Did she think Ann was asking too much of the tiny village, expecting someone to help her when everyone was working overtime to gather their own winter's supply of food? Ann knew she was, but what else could she do? Hopefully, someday, she would be able to return the kindness.

When May and Abner Gunther came that afternoon to drive her home, Ann was exhausted and in a completely foul mood. She had spent the waiting time hobbling back and forth on her crutches until her shoulders ached from the weight they were forced to bare. But it had been impossible to rest. There was trouble somewhere. She was too restless to just lie in the hospital bed and wait to find out what was wrong.

"Tell me what happened in Pinewood," Ann demanded, swinging out of the hospital room the minute the Gunthers arrived.

"My, you're in a rush," May said in her slow deliberate way.

"Aunt Eva is keeping something from me," Ann declared. "She didn't answer my questions and hung up in the middle of a sentence."

Looking at each other with their silent communication, neither Gunther spoke for agonizing seconds.

"Everything is fine," Abner finally answered. "This all your stuff?"

They won't tell me either, Ann thought. Calming her fears, Ann tried to be polite on the ride home. "Thanks for coming for me, I really appreciate your taking the time."

"Glad to do it. We had shopping to do anyway," May answered.

"I'll surely pay back whoever volunteered to help. Could Alma or Alice spare the time?"

"Someone will be there," Abner replied.

The rest of the trip was made in silence. It seemed pointless to continue asking questions for Ann was getting the same evasive answers she had gotten from her aunt. At least these two withdrawn friends didn't seem worried, in fact she had the suspicion they were amused. A ridiculous thought under the circumstances.

When they passed right by the Gilbert's home, Ann's surprise made her blurt out, "Aren't we going to pick up the twins?"

"They're already home," May answered.

Not until she was hobbling on her crutches up the front walk did Ann hear the conversation coming from inside her home.

"Will you stop playing with those babies and come help me with these damn diapers!" Rogers voice bellowed, vibrating off the log walls.

"You wanted this job," came back Seth's response, accompanied by a malicious chuckle.

Ann swung herself in the front door, followed by a now obviously amused Abner and May.

So this was why Aunt Eva had been so evasive. There was nothing wrong at all. The village just wanted to enjoy Ann's first reaction to the fact that Roger Anderson would be in charge of the Randall household.

Chapter 22

A disheveled head of black curly hair appeared coming from the bathroom, accompanied by a body holding a dripping bundle of clothes.

"Oh, you're home," Roger said sheepishly when he saw Ann standing in the doorway.

So this was the big secret. Roger, the important, wealthy television writer, who obviously knew nothing about running a home, was to be her savior. Not sweet Alma, nor dictatorial Alice nor even Mrs. Jones with her skill at avoiding work, but Roger Anderson. No wonder Abner and May were silently amused on the ride home.

"You are going to run this house?" Ann questioned in disbelief.

"Oh," Roger said, now aware that a puddle was gathering on the hardwood floor. "Just a minute, I've got to hang these up." He left trailing a stream of water out the back door all the way to the clothesline.

Ann collapsed in the nearest chair and silently glared at the three remaining adults. Seth, Abner and May were all smiling, in fact they were trying very hard not to laugh at her reaction to her new housekeeper.

"Don't you worry. The whole village will be here everyday." Seth grinned broadly. "We wouldn't miss this for the world."

"Roger running a house. I never thought I would see the day," Abner said. Now unable to contain his laughter, he burst forth with such exuberance he had to sit down.

Poor Roger, Ann thought suddenly. He's so kind to offer to help and here they are thinking it's the biggest joke of the year. Though he did look pretty funny with that load of washed diapers dripping down his pant legs, he must have forgotten to use the wringer or perhaps didn't know how.

Roger returned with that delightful smile on his face. A little boy smile of pleasure, Ann thought, wondering why it was so appealing.

"Well, that's done, thank goodness. What's next?" he asked.

"Dinner," Seth reminded him.

"Oh, yes. Let's see. The fish you caught, Seth, my mom's baked beans and fresh string beans from Ann's garden. Sound okay to everyone?"

"We aren't staying," May Gunther remarked. "Abner and I have chores to do."

"Just show me how to fix the beans before you go, will you, May?"

"Hum," May said, looking around for freshly picked string beans.

"I'll pick some beans," Abner said, noticing they were nowhere in sight and should be started before the fish was cooked. Going to the back door with a bowl, he added, "That is, after I rehang those diapers. Roger you can't just throw them over the line, they'll never dry."

"How then?" Roger asked, still immensely cheerful.

"Come on, I'll show you."

Both Seth and Ann watched as May set the table for five. Giving Ann a wink, Seth broke into a silent smile.

Somehow, not only did the Gunthers stay for dinner but they were still there well after all the chores were finished. Only when Abner insisted, did May reluctantly leave but not before she had given Roger explicit instructions for his morning duties.

When the babies were settled for the night and Ann had just herself to care for, Seth and Roger left. She wanted to ask Roger why he was doing this, why he was taking care of her home and family. But she was too exhausted to ask. The need to collapse on her own bed and sleep for hours was overpowering.

"Well, we made it through the first day," he had said proudly, just before leaving. "Tomorrow you can help with the canning. There are bushels of string beans out there. I'll set you up at the table and you can chop away while I do the other chores."

What confidence, Ann thought, as if he had done all the work himself. Without May, Abner and Seth he would still by trying to get dinner on the table. But she couldn't help smiling when she thought of the day. Roger had looked so pleased with himself. Was he really that inept at housekeeping or was the proximity of so much good help too much of a temptation for him to resist. I'll find out in the next few weeks, she reasoned, before allowing herself to fall asleep.

Waking to the faint sound of humming, Ann's sleepy brain tried to recall the song. "Someone's Singing Lord, Kumba yah," of course, "Come By Here."

Groping in the faint light she tried to read her watch. Five-thirty! Five-thirty in the morning and Roger was already here working at something. She could hear running water and the incessant humming of that beautiful song. Well, if he can be cheerful this early in the morning, so can I, she decided, easing her plastered leg over the side of the bed.

Her sleeveless night gown had added numerous wrinkles during the night, her long curly black hair hung over her eyes and because of the medication her teeth felt as if they hadn't been brushed in a week. Opening the louvered door of the closet, Ann selected her roomiest pair of cut off jeans and a loose fitting shirt. Trying to be unconcerned with Roger's reaction to her early morning appearance, she hobbled off to the privacy of the bathroom.

"Good morning," Roger said, stirring something on the stove.

"Hum," she answered not looking up, knowing from the sound of his voice, he was enjoying the scene immensely. He will be worn out and bored by the end of the day, Ann told herself, keeping up her guard. Forgetting for a moment the feel of his strong competent hands as he wrapped her broken leg. The relief and joy she had known when she had heard his words, "It will be all right, love."

An hour later they sat down to oatmeal, toast and

blackberry jelly, Roger helping baby Sally while Ann cared for little Eva. Roger had spent the previous hour bathing and dressing the twins. The laughter and giggling coming from the bathroom and the appearance of two toddlers properly dressed assuring Ann that he at least knew how to care for children.

Ann had spent the time experimenting with what she could accomplish. Bed making was out but she could prop herself against the kitchen counter, slice bread, gather dishes and silverware and later be able to prepare vegetables.

"This is like living my dream," Roger said, smiling shyly while spreading the dark purple jelly over a piece of toast. "Ever since I read my first pioneer book, I fantasized myself living in a log cabin with my very own family."

Ann's heart softened, he seemed so sincere. Could it be that this was important to him, spending time with ordinary, daily family living?

"Roger, I'm ever so grateful. If you hadn't come when you did, we might all be dead. The girls couldn't have survived that burning sun during the day nor the cold night dressed in just their play suits."

"Hush, love, it didn't happen. You're all safe."

"Because of you. But why are you taking charge of my house? Surely the village women could take turns helping me."

"This is a heaven sent opportunity to prove something to you, my stubborn little friend."

"What? That you're a nice person? I already know that."

"You do! Good, we are getting somewhere." Roger said with a smile. "But to answer your question. I'm washing diapers, cooking meals, feeding chickens and hoeing your garden to prove to you that your life is as important to me as my own. I'm trying to dispel your fears that men don't care about children, family life or being faithful."

"You didn't sound too happy about washing diapers. When I came home yesterday, I heard a bit of swearing," Ann challenged.

"True, there are parts of this responsibility I'm not crazy about, but over all I'm a very happy guy and I expect to be even happier in the future." Roger answered, giving Ann a loving look that sent her heart racing.

Their eyes met and held. For a moment time stopped. Slowly Roger rose and started around the table. She knew he was going to take her in his arms and she knew she would welcome his embrace. Half way around the table he stopped, forcefully controlling his emotions. Shifting his gaze to the twins, he remained silent, deep in thought. Ann had no idea what was going through his mind.

Some moments passed before he gave her a wistful smile and said, "The string beans, onward with the beans."

Because the day promised to be in the seventies, clear and bright with little wind, Roger moved his adopted family outdoors. He set up boards on two old saw horses, giving Ann a place to sit and prepare the vegetables for canning, with the play pen nearby so that she could talk to the children while she worked. By the time their first caller arrived, the assembly line was well underway. Roger picking, Ann cleaning and cutting and the jars being sterilized in boiling water on the kitchen stove.

Alice Ruffles came around the house carrying a chair which she set at Ann's make shift table. Her leathery face had a serious, subdued expression. Seating herself, she asked softly, "What would you like me to do?"

Ann couldn't believe her ears. All the time she had lived in Pinewood she had never heard Alice ask for directions. Giving directions was her specialty.

"Alice are you all right?" Ann couldn't help asking.

"Of course!" The village's gray haired general bristled as she perceptibly straightened her spine. "Just tell me how I can help."

"The jars should be sterilized by now. If you will bring them out here, I can pack them with beans and we can get the first batch in the pressure cooker," Ann said, still wondering what had produced this change in Alice Ruffles.

While Alice was in the cabin, Roger came to the table with two more pails of beans.

"Alice actually asked me what to do! She didn't barge in and take charge!" Ann informed him, expecting Roger to be equally amazed.

Roger just smiled and went back to the garden.

Together Ann and Alice put the prepared beans into the canning jars.

"My, he is a forceful young man," Alice whispered, watching Roger pick yet more string beans. "I had everything all planned. Alma was going to help you on Mondays, May on Tuesdays, Eva on Wednesdays, with Seth bringing Albert over in his truck so he could see the twins. Mrs. Jones on Thursdays, though I doubt she would be much help, Mrs. Jacobson on Fridays and Sara Woodbind on Saturdays. Sara is always glad to get out of the house on Saturdays. The

Reverend drives her up the wall when he is preparing his sermons, stomps around the house muttering to himself and bumping into anything in his path. Naturally I would take Sundays, make sure you got to church and had a good wholesome meal afterwards.

But do you know what Roger did? He absolutely refused our help! He said he was taking charge, that he would be here everyday and no one was to interfere with his authority. Can you imagine that! I have never seen such a determined young man in my life. I was almost afraid to come over today. But then I thought, I had better make sure he isn't making a mess of everything."

The thought of Alice Ruffles being maneuvered into a subservient position brought a smile to Ann's face. Quickly ducking her head over the beans, Ann tried to keep her expression from view.

This was a side of Roger Ann had never seen. To think that he could calmly stand up to Alice Ruffles, in one of her command, take charge moods and actually dominate this woman, was amazing. The rest of the little town had long since given in and now meekly followed Alice's directions whenever there was need for village organization.

Ann had been acutely aware of Roger's kindness and empathy during Sally's last visit. She had seen his need to withdraw into a private world and his fun loving abandonment at the swimming hole. But this description of a strong dominant personality intrigued her. If they did marry - a big if in her mind - there would be battles, for she had developed a strong determined streak herself. And yet with a man like Roger she would feel protected.

That night when she wrote to Sally Canfield,

describing her accident and all that followed, she closed with:

"No doubt Roger will soon tire, be all too eager to return to the excitement of Hollywood. But in the meantime I am grateful for his help. There is comfort in having a man about the house. More than that, really, there is a feeling of completeness, as if God intended it to be this way. I would love to have him take me in his arms, but I know if he did I would be lost. All my resolve to be free, to keep this protective wall around myself would crumble."

Because of Ann's accident the plans for the twins and Jimmy Junior's birthday party had been altered. Originally Ann was to have had the celebration at her log cabin, but now all were to gather at Aunt Eva's house directly after church on Sunday. The entire congregation was invited for a pot luck picnic with birthday cake to follow. Fortunately, the weather, now in its pleasant fall glory, held true to form; sunny and dry with a deep blue sky and only a few yellow leaves to remind the village of what was to come.

Sally Canfield's mother had sent two adorable pale pink dresses for this important event. With Roger's help, Ann dressed the twins in their ruffled finery.

"My, what beauties you are!" he said, buckling them in his sports car. "Steal the heart of any man, you will." Giggles were the response to his flattering words.

The party was a huge success. Neighbors who had barely seen each other throughout the busy harvest season, caught up on the news. Mr. McLaughlin, one of their snow birds, brought along a camera and happily took pictures of the birthday trio; one of Jimmy Junior and the twins with a pink and blue decorated birthday cake in the foreground, one of the twins sitting on Uncle Albert's lap and several pictures of both families.

All three babies were held, admired and given a gigantic supply of attention. Even Mrs. Jones took a turn cuddling baby Eva. The look of joy on her face when she held the baby made Ann wonder if the old woman was really lonely and that was perhaps why she gave the village such a hard time. Maybe she should invite Mrs. Jones down someday, let her spend time with the twins. Surely it wouldn't change her stingy ways, but it might help her to be a happier person.

Hot dogs and hamburgers were grilled over charcoal and served with a variety of rolls, a range of brightly colored jello molds and bowls of cut up fresh fruit. Each birthday child was given a piece of cake with one lighted candle protruding above the frosting. With a little help from a nearby adult, all three candles were extinguished, amid cheers and flashing cameras.

Sufficiently nourished, the Pinewood residents relaxed in lawn chairs or rested on the grass. Overall a happy, contented group. The harvest, an exceptionally good one, was winding down. Each home larder was filled to capacity, some even overflowing, so that those who still had apple sauce and plums to preserve were wondering where to find extra storage space. With a summer of sufficient rain and unusually warm weather, the fruit and vegetables were not only abundant, but large and succulent, resulting in a comfortable feeling of security and work well done. Their young mother's broken leg was mending well and the three junior members of the village were rosy cheeked, healthy children with much promise. The only sadness was the loss of Marie and Wilber Burton, so recently taken from their midst.

"How is Wilber adjusting to the nursing home?"

May asked Alice Ruffles. Alice always made it a point to visit Wilber whenever she attended a county board meeting in Hendersonville.

"He is doing better now, even taking part in some of the activities. He won a new wallet in the weekly bingo game and was quite thrilled. Had to show it to me the minute I went into his room."

"And the children?" The villagers plied Alice with questions, knowing she had sources of information.

"That is a mess. The two boys tried to run away and Gretta has become completely withdrawn. She won't talk to anyone."

"Oh dear. Can't something be done?" Phyllis asked.

"The social workers are hoping they will adjust, in time. The children are in a home in the city. It must be overwhelming for them, with all the people, traffic and just a small yard to play in," Alice replied in a resigned tone of voice.

The thought that they hadn't found any relatives who might take the children went through everyone's mind, for the villagers were well aware that Alice would have informed them had there been any word.

As there was nothing the group could do about the Burton, Sweeney situation, other than visit Wilber whenever they were in Hendersonville, they wisely changed the topic of conversation. For this was a birthday celebration, a time for joy and thankfulness.

Chapter 23

The fall weeks sped by. Ann would soon have her cast removed and Roger would be free from daily chores. Over the six weeks they had settled into a comfortable working relationship almost to the point of reading each other's mind. Few words were needed for they had grown to anticipate plans and actions. Often when something amusing or mildly disastrous happened, a glass of spilled milk or a broken shoe lace, they would automatically look at each other and smile, communicating silently with their eyes.

One evening, a full moon crept over the horizon lighting up the quiet countryside with almost daylight brightness. The twins had just fallen asleep, Roger was stacking wood for the fire in preparation for leaving, Ann, drawn to the outside splendor, went out in the back yard.

"Unbelievable size when it first comes up," Roger said, joining her.

"Isn't that fiery orange color impressive? The harvest moon seems to dominate everything. You can't help but be awed by its magnificence."

"In Hollywood you are hardly ever aware of the moon or the stars for that matter, too many human made distractions.

When I was a kid I daydreamed of living like this, close to the natural world. I read every homesteading book in the library; the ones I liked I even read three or four times. After the farm house burned down and Mom moved to the village, I started building my dream."

"Why did you leave? You had the cabin and the land, the fulfillment of your fantasies."

"Money. My works were not selling. I was slowly beginning to starve. Except for Mom bringing over casseroles, I probably would have. Anyway, a friend of mine suggested I come out to Hollywood and try writing for T.V. I saw it as a quick way to pick up some capital, so I gave it a try. Within a few weeks I got the job of writing for "Loves of My Life." Once the show became popular I was well on my way to making a fortune, or at least a fortune by Northern Wisconsin standards." Roger explained.

"Is that when you decided to give up your dream and sell the log cabin?"

"At first it is intoxicating to have lots of money. You find yourself looking at everything and saying to yourself, "I can buy one of these and one of those." And you do. You buy a fancy car, you rent an expensive apartment and you go everywhere. Soon you're working just to have the means to buy all the things you want or think you want. Your work becomes a way to have more possessions, losing all significance in its own right.

Then one day a poor little girl buys your dream and sends you homemade jelly in a reused mayonnaise jar. You spread it on a piece of toast one morning and all those years of growing up free to roam the woods, fish in the lakes and watch Canadian Geese fly over, come back. Suddenly you know where you really belong and what you should be doing. That big empty feeling in your soul leaves just as you start packing your bags."

"You went back to Hollywood this summer," Ann said accusingly, recalling how hurt she had been when he didn't tell her he was leaving.

"I went back to resign for good."

Roger turned and gently put a hand on each of her cheeks. Holding her head so she had to meet his eyes, he said softly, "I knew the minute I met that little jelly maker she was meant for me. Meant to be my life long companion, my love, my wife."

He brought his lips to hers and kissed her gently. When he released her, he said, "Did you know my book, our book will be published this winter?" Even if it doesn't make a lot of money, I now know I can write about the things that really concern me and be published."

"It's a very good book, Roger."

"Thanks, but it isn't the kind of book that brings in a fortune."

"Does that matter?" Ann asked.

"Not in the least."

"Roger," Ann said hesitantly, "You say you want to

give up the excitement of a metropolitan area, live a quiet country life. But in time won't it seem dull? Won't you miss the variety of people, the intellectual stimulation of constantly meeting new minds and the endless new places to go? Won't you find the world that was exciting to a ten year old, boring to an adult?"

"Ann," he said, looking off into the shadows cast by the rising moon. A soft black and white world. After a pause, seeming to organize his thoughts he carefully continued. "I'm a very private person. I need hours and hours just being alone, talking to God, allowing my thoughts to crystallize. I also need the natural world: the trees, the lakes, the flowers, the view from a hill top, the deer feeding on the edge of an open field, the squirrels circling around a tree trunk. They're all part of me. I can't think, feel, survive without them. Ann, I lost touch with God. I became so dominated by material things and other people I just forgot about Him. Slowly my life was going sour and I didn't know why. But once you reminded me of home; of those years of talking to God in our little Pinewood church and during walks in the woods, everything came back to me and I knew, without a doubt, what was missing in my life. I'm just so grateful that God had patience with me."

"How have you managed these past six weeks, coming here everyday and being surrounded by people dependent on you?"

"This is different. This is my family. I'm in love with all three of you. But just so you'll know the real me; after I leave here I take long solitary walks."

Ann folded her arms and leaned against the corner of the log cabin, still watching the rising moon.

"Roger, when I first saw you with that sopping wet load of diapers, I thought you wouldn't last a week as a housekeeper. I was wrong. You proved to me that you do care about a home and a family, that they are important to you. In fact, you seem to have your life in order, to know exactly what you want and where you're going. I wish I could say the same thing about myself."

The following morning they dropped the twins at Aunt Eva's home and drove to Hendersonville. The big cast removing ceremony was to take place at the clinic. Ann could hardly wait for Doctor Durand to saw off the stiff plaster as at times the itching had been unbearable. She longed to soak her leg in a tub of hot water, removing the perspiration and dirt that had piled up over the last six weeks.

To keep her mind from the itching Ann asked Roger about his mother. "Why hasn't Alma been over to see us? The rest of the village drops in just about everyday. I think we have been the height of entertainment for the past six weeks. Everyone must have knocked themselves out getting their canning done so they could watch you run a house."

"Oh, Mother doesn't dare come," Roger replied, beginning to smile. "She's so afraid of being too possessive."

"Too possessive? She doesn't seem like the possessive type." Ann said, looking perplexed.

"She isn't. But, remember I am an only child and Dad died years ago. Her greatest fear has been that she will become a stifling mother who clings to her only child. Or a bossy possessive one who not only dominates her child, but his wife and family as well. She has read so many articles on the subject, she is paranoid. When I was growing up she practically threw me at any man in the village who offered to take me fishing or hunting. The result was I hunted two years before any other boy in Pinewood was allowed near a gun. Now that I look back I know she was worried sick, but she never would let on. That is why the hands off rule now. Even when we do see her there won't be a drop of advice given. Just ask her a question and all you will hear is, 'I don't know dear, whatever you think best'."

Really, she is not that kind of person at all, actually she is very positive and determined about her own life."

"What a shame," Ann said. "I do like her immensely. There are times I would rather have her company than yours."

Roger laughed. "I'll tell her that. Maybe it will help her to be more natural. She likes you too, has from the first time you met. The delivery of, "Under Protest," if I remember the story correctly. Naturally she didn't even hint that I might find you attractive - the old, don't meddle code - but I knew that look in her eye, she could hardly wait for us to meet."

Doctor Durand was extremely busy. They had to wait in the overcrowded reception room with its old magazines, fussing sick children and other restless occupants.

The room was antiseptically clean, smelling of a strong disinfectant. The walls were white and the straight chairs were covered in a washable black plastic. A room you would never spend time in unless you had no other choice.

Almost every adult glanced at his watch, looked around the room with uninterested eyes and sighed on the average of every ten minutes. Mothers with sick children showed signs of concern, mixed with fatigue.

After what seemed like hours, Ann could thankfully put down the old magazine she had been thumbing through for the third time and follow the nurse into one of the cubicles, which was equally white, antiseptic, but this time claustrophobic, leaving Roger pretending to be engrossed in an article on deep sea fishing.

Another boring wait and Doctor Durand burst into the room, cheerfully pleasant, undaunted by the crowded waiting room. Regardless of the fact that it meant he would be late for dinner, again.

"So anxious to get that cast off, I suppose. It does look a bit ratty," he remarked.

"I practically scratched through it."

"Well, don't break your leg and you won't have that problem. Did you bring my apples? I may not cut this off unless I get paid."

"Boy, are you sympathetic," Ann laughed. "We have them in Roger's car. We will deliver the apples to your very front door step, once I'm free."

"Not above a bit of bribery yourself, I see," Doctor Durand kidded, enjoying the banter with a patient now restored to good health.

A few minutes of the whine of a specialized saw and Ann was looking at wrinkled white skin. An application of ointment and she was once again whole and unencumbered.

"Thanks, doctor, you are not a bad sort at all," Ann said gratefully. Knowing any more flowery phasing of her appreciation would embarrass the good doctor.

"That is what I tell all my patients. Now you take it easy young lady. Your twins are my only delivery of a pair in ten years, make sure you take excellent care of them."

Chapter 24

By one o'clock the next day Ann was missing Roger terribly. His smile when he came in from the garden, his jolly laugh when he played with the twins, even his occasional, "Damn," when things went wrong.

Usually when people left, as much as she adored them, Ann didn't mind being alone. Even her partings from Sally Canfield, as close friends as they were, left her with mixed feelings. Loneliness and loss surely, but also a feeling of being free to think her own thoughts, work at her own pace and no longer be responsible for the comfort of another.

But Roger was different; he had become part of the family. A vitally important part that left a huge void with his absence. She could be completely herself with Roger: go off into her own world almost forgetting he was there, work closely with him on some project, their minds so in tune they hardly had to speak, or get into a lively discussion that sent their thoughts racing, full of stimulation and creativity.

It's obvious I'm in love, Ann thought. Nothing he does annoys me, every little habit he has is dear.

The early afternoon when the babies were down for their nap proved to be the hardest period of all. Roger had taken to bringing his writing pad and while Ann knitted mittens or caps for the coming winter they had discussed his writing; perhaps arrangement of a sentence or the idea a paragraph conveyed. In order not to wake the babies with their conversation, Ann had moved her chair near the desk. Close enough to see the frown on his face and the way he ran his fingers through his black curly hair when he was mentally searching for the right word, the way his muscles tensed, bulging under his thin tee shirt, when the thought he wanted came to his conscious mind and the way he wrote with his left hand, rapid concise movements with his fist curved to the right.

Alone for the first time in weeks, Ann cast on thirty stitches, ten on each needle and started knitting one, purling one, for the second of a pair of mittens. Finishing the ribbing, she had no desire to continue. Placing her knitting on the table she checked to see that the babies were comfortable. Assured that they were sound asleep, she quietly went out the back door to wander around the yard, too restless to have any desire to work on a project.

The fall leaves were at their height of splendor. Yellows, rusts, golds and reds all mixed together and highlighted by the deep greens of spruce and pines. The overcast sky seemed to heighten the fall brilliance as if keeping the bright sun from dimming their glory. She wandered past the chicken coup where a few birds were leisurely scratching, climbed the small hill beyond the apple trees and looked at the panoramic view the slight rise afforded. Beauty was everywhere, a gorgeous display. Ann could turn full circle and be met on every side by the stimulating grandeur of fall. The crisp clean air coming down from Canada added to her feeling of invigoration.

Surely, surrounded by God's magnificent world, she could dare to dream again. Dare to take risks, to grow with His will to guide her.

Glancing back toward her home with its dark brown solid logs, now surrounded by blazing reds, sparkling yellows and soft rusts, Ann saw a new gold colored Blazer pull into the yard adding to the panorama of color. Surprisingly, Roger climbed out and hurried toward the house. In a few minutes he came out the back door, looking around, obviously trying to find her.

Waving from her hill top, Ann called, "Roger."

Hearing his name, Roger glanced her way then ran up the hill. His face was dead serious, his eyes penetrating and intense. Ann had just time to wonder what was wrong when he said, "To heck with this." Grasping her firmly in his arms, crushing her to himself, his lips found hers. He kissed her with passion, causing her heart to race with a feeling of being fully awake, fully alive.

"Do you love me?" he demanded, holding her tightly against his solid muscular chest.

"Oh, yes!"

"Tell me about your husband. I have to know why

you've built up this wall. Why you've been keeping me out."

"I'm not sure you'll understand."

With his arm still around her, Roger guided Ann to a comfortable spot where they could sit, resting their backs against a tree trunk.

"Try me," was all he said.

Slowly Ann composed herself, trying to put her feelings into words that Roger might understand. "Tom was a fun loving person: he adored parties, going places, having a good time. When we were first married everything was great, we joked, we laughed, we danced until midnight. We thought it would go on forever. Even after we decided to save money for a house things were still okay until I got pregnant. Then everything fell apart. We found we had completely different ideas about raising a family. It was as if once life became serious, we had no common ground, no trust. All of a sudden our lives together were built on sand.

At first I blamed Tom and then I blamed myself, but the simple truth was our marriage had fallen apart and if he had lived it would have been a broken relationship, existing without true meaning. Roger, I'm afraid! I'm afraid of making mistakes."

"Darling, our marriage will be before God. We'll ask God to guide us and help us with every decision. It's when we forget God that the big mistakes are made. We'll trust God and we'll have faith that our love will blossom and grow. Ann, you're precious to me. I want to protect and care for you and the girls and cherish you always."

"Oh, Roger. I do so need your love, your strength and your wisdom."

"I adore you," he said, brushing his lips across Ann's cheek. "Will you marry me and let me prove every word I've said?"

"Yes, oh yes. You've become such a part of us, we couldn't live without you. I love you dearly." As Ann answered she suddenly felt that God approved, that somehow she and Roger were meant to be together.

Their kiss was a giving, a release of desires long held in restraint.

How wonderful it felt to let go of her self imposed wall, to be free again to trust. Ann gently pulled away. "There is just one more thing," she said. "You spoke of being separated from God when you were in Hollywood. I've also felt a distance from God, at times. Even though I thought I was doing everything right: caring for my children, providing a home, going to church, in other words following all the rules. But in those troubled times I didn't turn to God for help and guidance and in my heart I wasn't forgiving myself and Tom, I was holding onto the hurt and fear. But now I'm free, free to love you and our family with all my heart."

"Let's wake up the girls and go check in with Reverend Woodbind," Roger said huskily, as he kissed her forehead, cheeks and lips.

"After the Reverend, let's go see Seth," Ann whispered. "He has been hinting that I marry you for the past three months."

"Has he, by jove! I should have known I could count on my old hunting buddy."

They bundled the girls into Roger's new Blazer, the proper type of vehicle for country living, according to Roger. Reverend Woodbind and Sara were delighted with their news and joyously made plans for the wedding.

When they arrived at the Ruffle farm they found Seth in his garden digging the last of his potatoes. He was mighty pleased with the news, though in his usual caustic manner his only comment was, "It's about time." But the way his eyes sparkled and the joyous grin on his ugly face said more than words. When Roger asked him to be his best man, the grin broadened to a smile.

"Come on the porch," Seth offered. "We can better discuss this here big event over a cup of coffee."

Seth's wide front porch, built low to the ground with a two foot railing, extended across the front of the white farm house. It contained four assorted chairs in various stages of decay. From the porch Ann could see the red barn and beyond, rolling hills dotted with black and white grazing milk cows. The front door led directly into a kitchen surprisingly modern, with a gas stove, refrigerator and ruffled curtains on the windows.

"Alice's doings," Seth said when Ann stared at the white ruffles on the windows.

Seth's contribution to the room was fifty years of household accumulation, including an old metal coffee pot. Ann watched as he poured water in the pot, dumped in coffee grounds without measuring, added an egg including the shell and put this concoction on the stove. Next he took assorted mugs from an overhead cupboard, cream and sugar still in their original containers and one stirring spoon and put these necessities on an old metal tray. The process finally completed, they sat on the porch allowing the coffee grounds to settle to the bottom of their mugs.

It was the strongest coffee Ann had ever tasted. Wondering whether it would be best to drink it quickly or slowly, Ann decided on slowly, quickly might mean refusing a second cup. Now she knew why Seth did favors in return for home cooked meals.

"Best man, well, well. I haven't been a best man since back in the forties. You don't mind if I wear the same suit, do you? It still fits and has hardly had any use since then."

"Wear whatever you like," Roger replied smiling. "I'm not going to be looking at you anyway. I have my angel to gaze upon. Unless you drop the ring, I won't even know you're in the church."

"Don't tell me that, young fella." Seth chuckled. "You'll be so nervous you'll be asking my advice every second."

"Don't say that in front of Ann. I want her to think I am strong, brave, courageous and invincible."

"Of course I think those wonderful things about you, dear," Ann said, joining in the fun.

"If it weren't for me singing your praises, you wouldn't be thinking about my dropping the ring," Seth embellished. "Yes sir, I deserve a lot of credit for getting you two together. My, I sure do! Should be worth at least one dinner a week. At least one."

"You help me add on to the log cabin and maybe my good wife will consider your bold hint."

Ann looked at Seth with a broad loving smile. "Seth, you old manipulator. You're a part of our family whether you want to be or not. There is no way out."

"Well in that case, who are we inviting to the wedding? That Sally friend of yours, I hope," Seth said with a grin.

"I'll ask Sally to be my maid of honor and Phyllis Westland to be my bride's maid. And do let's invite the entire church congregation."

"I have some Hollywood friends I would like to ask. Especially the ones who think Wisconsin is the perfect state," Roger offered.

"Oh, yes, there is Tom's brother and his family," Ann added.

Seth poured himself another cup of coffee. As he did so, he spoke slowly and seriously, "There are few more Ruffles in Hendersonville I should include. Maybe forty or fifty is all. They ain't all Ruffles, some are married to Ruffles and some are Ruffle kids who now have different names."

Roger and Ann couldn't tell whether Seth was kidding or not and both hesitated to ask, though the guest list was now reaching alarming proportions.

The view from the porch was pleasantly restful in spite of the conversation. Situated on the top of a rise, the location gave a commanding view of grazing hills, the dirt road winding off in the distance and further afield, the beginning of a pine forest. They could see Alice Ruffles' car approaching along the curved road long before she pulled up at the farm house.

Chapter 25

"I'm glad you're all here," she said, alighting from the car. Breathlessly she came onto the porch, adding as she sat in the one remaining chair, "The most awful thing has happened! The social agency is breaking up the Sweeney family. They're going to allow Will and his brother to be adopted. Some nice family that lives out in the country, I hear. But that means Gretta will have to stay in that foster home all by herself."

"There is no possibility that relatives will take the children?" Ann asked.

"No, no." They've given up on trying to find any. Whatever we do, we mustn't tell Wilber. This news would just about kill him," Alice added.

"Coffee, Alice," her brother offered.

"Half coffee and half hot water and I'll take it," Alice agreed. "I need something to help me with the shock of this one. Poor little Gretta, first she loses her home, now she's losing her brothers."

Returning with Alice's coffee, Seth placed it in his sister's hands and picked up baby Sally. Holding his adored godchild he looked solemnly at Ann.

Ann looked at Roger. A silent communication passed between them.

"We could ———?" Ann half questioned.

"Definitely," Roger answered.

"Add one of your own and you'll have, 'Little Women'," Seth joined in.

"Whatever are you three talking about?" Alice demanded.

She did not appreciate the laughter that greeted her remark. For Seth, Ann and Roger had been working so closely together that they had come to know each other's thoughts. The idea that Ann and Roger could adopt Gretta, had crossed each mind at the same time, resulting in little need for words.

"These two love birds are going to bring Gretta back home," Seth said, putting his sister out of her misery.

"You mean you're getting married! How splendid!" Alice cried. "And you're going to adopt Gretta and bring her back to Pinewood. That is absolutely perfect! Simply perfect! But what about room? That cabin isn't big enough for, well, it isn't very big."

"As soon as Ann approves the plans, Seth, Abner and I will start the addition. We should have it roofed in before winter arrives," Roger assured her. "I'm afraid we'll have to add a few modern conveniences too. With the size our family is going to be, we will need appliances to help with the daily chores."

After more discussion of where to find the necessary trees for the new addition, wedding plans and how to contact Gretta's social worker, Roger, Ann and the babies left to tell Aunt Eva and Uncle Albert their joyous news.

That night Ann rested on her bed, with the soft glow of a kerosene lamp lighting up the pages of a long letter from Sally Canfield. The twins were sleeping peacefully in their crib, soft rosy cheeks shining in the dim light.

Ann read:

> The most marvelous news! I have been promoted to vice president, with a salary increase that will put me close to a hundred thousand a year. Isn't that the most divine news! I would have called immediately instead of writing but YOU DON'T HAVE A PHONE - hint, hint.
>
> Mother is all aglow with my success but still disappointed that there are no grandchildren in her future. I am so intrigued with business, I've given no thought to marriage. What I'll do is marry Jimmy Burns when I'm sixty-five, after the excitement of being a high powered executive has worn off.
>
> To think we were pounding typewriters in a dingy office for five dollars an hour just a little over a year ago. Can you believe it, Ann? Now here

I am about to make a hundred
thousand dollars a year and you have
two adorable babies, your own home
and are about to marry that fantastic
Roger Anderson. If I'm not mistaken.

To celebrate my becoming a V.P.,
Mom and I are running up to Pinewood
next weekend. Couldn't think of
celebrating without you.

Ann immediately wrote back.

Dearest Sally,

I'm so proud of you! What simply
magnificent news! Are you going to buy
your first Mercedes from Honest
Freddie?

Your timing for the weekend is
perfect. Bring your best bib and tucker,
for I won't have my wedding without
you. Yes, (you were so right!) Roger and
I will marry next weekend when you
and your mom are here. I'm absolutely
in heaven for I not only adore Roger, I
know this marriage is right with God.
Tell Mother Canfield not to worry. We
will name our second girl after her. The
first one will be named Alma, but your
mom is in line for the next, unless of
course, you and Jimmy —————-.